VAMPS

NANCY A. COLLINS

HARPER TEEN

AN IMPRINT OF HARPERCOLLINS*PUBLISHERS*

HarperTeen is an imprint of HarperCollins Publishers.

Vamps

Library of Congress Cataloging-in-Publication Data
Collins, Nancy A.
    Vamps / by Nancy A. Collins. — 1st ed.
        p.   cm.
    Summary: At an elite vampire prep school in Manhattan,
sixteen-year-old vampire socialite Lilith seeks revenge against
Cally, a new student and "New Blood" Lilith holds responsible
for the death of her close friend during a dispute that attracted
heavily armed Van Helsings.
    ISBN 978-0-06-134917-1 (pbk.)
    [1. Vampires—Fiction. 2. Social classes—Fiction. 3.
Wealth—Fiction. 4. Schools—Fiction. 5. Manhattan (New
York, N.Y.)—Fiction.] I. Title.
PZ7.C683528Vam   2008   2007038746
[Fic]—dc22   CIP
                                                        AC

Typography by Andrea Vandergrift

❖

First Edition

*In loving memory of my aunt, Emily Riggins,
and with special thanks to my agent, Lori Perkins,
and my editor, Barbara Lalicki*

What a strange illusion it is
to suppose that beauty is goodness.
—Leo Tolstoy

CHAPTER 1

"You can drop me off here, Bruno," Lilith Todd said as she slid a Christian Louboutin heel onto her right foot.

The chauffeur quickly glanced over his shoulder at her as he piloted the vintage Rolls along Sixth Avenue. Bruno had been driving the Todd family to and from their various destinations since the days of cobblestones and coach-and-fours. Before that he'd been an officer in some European army.

He asked, "Are you sure, Miss Lilith? I can drive around the block one more time if you like."

Lilith checked to make sure her backless emerald-green Dior dress was zipped to the waist and glanced at her Patek Philippe watch. She was secretly pleased to see she had broken her personal best for changing from her school uniform into her party clothes in the back of the limo.

"I said *now*, Bruno."

"Yes, Miss Lilith."

As the driver stopped at the club in the section cordoned off for valet service, a young man dressed in the Belfry's standard-issue black designer pants, T-shirt, and dinner jacket hurried up to open the car door.

The Belfry was once an Episcopal church built by robber barons. More than 125 years later, the rich and famous still streamed through its ornate double doors; only now they came to minister to the flesh and drink the spirit.

Even though it was after two in the morning, there were plenty of wannabes hanging around, grumbling among themselves and eyeing the beefy bouncers guarding the entrance to the club. As Lilith extended a shapely leg onto the curb, the throng on the wrong side of the velvet ropes turned toward her, hungry for a glimpse, no matter how fleeting, of celebrity glamour.

With a toss of her head, Lilith moved up the stairs to the door, her long, honey-blond hair floating behind her like a bridal veil. One of the bridge-and-tunnel rats elbowed her companion in the ribs and pointed at Lilith as she breezed by.

"Look! There's someone famous! Isn't she . . . ?"

"I don't think so," her friend said, squinting like a jewel appraiser trying to tell the difference between a precious and semiprecious stone. "Too young. But I'm pretty sure she's someone famous. Or she's rich. Maybe both."

Lilith brought her hand to her mouth so that no one could see her laugh. Oh, she was rich and famous, all right. Just not in the way the wannabes were thinking.

As she reached the front door of the club, a new bouncer stretched out a bulging arm, blocking her way.

"You look the part, lady," he said, his eyes traveling up and down her svelte body. "But I need to see some ID."

Suddenly the valet ran up and tapped the bouncer on the shoulder. The huge mountain of man-muscle lowered his head so the valet could whisper into his ear. Lilith smiled as she saw the panic cross his face.

"Sorry, my mistake," the bouncer rumbled, exposing his throat in deference as he stepped out of her way. "Enjoy your night, Miss Todd."

Lilith crossed the glowing entryway and headed toward the massive main dance floor that filled what had once been the church sanctuary. She looked up at the DJ booth housed in the old pulpit and waved at the young man spinning trance at deafening levels.

She spotted Sebastian, the club's party promoter and appointed guardian of the VIP lounge on the second floor. He rushed toward her as fast as his custom-made blue leather shoes could carry him. As always, he was ecstatic to see her.

"Lilith! Baby! You look positively *ravishing*! It's *so*

good to see you!" he shouted over the throbbing punch of the club's sound system.

"Hello, Seb," she yelled back. "Are the others here?"

"Jules just arrived. Go on up to the Loft; I have your favorite vintage warmed and ready for you."

"You're my favorite, Seb!" she said, kissing the air to either side of his thin cheeks.

"I'm sure you say that to *all* the devilishly handsome club promoters who let you drink for free!" He winked.

As she entered the former choir loft that served as the VIP lounge for the club, Lilith spotted her promised, Jules de Laval, sprawled on one of the divans. He was dressed in an Armani polo T-shirt, the sleeves rolled up to give his biceps maximum reveal, chatting with Tanith Graves, one of her best friends. With his tousled, collar-length strawberry-blond hair, green eyes, perfectly straight nose, and strong masculine jaw, Jules looked like a movie star and loved to act the part.

Tanith and Lilith enjoyed passing for sisters, and since both girls had blond hair, oval faces, fake tans, and the same taste in high-end fashion, it was an easy con to pull off.

Sitting next to Tanith was her boyfriend, Sergei Savanovic, one of Jules's classmates from Ruthven's. With his dark, shoulder-length hair, black eyes, and penchant for turtleneck sweaters and leather jeans,

Sergei could easily be mistaken for a Russian poet, but he was actually from Serbia, as he was quick to point out to anyone who bothered to ask.

Carmen Duivel and Oliver Drake were sprawled on the opposite sofa. Carmen's baby-doll face and coppery tresses perfectly complemented Oliver's dirty blond hair and bad-boyish good looks. Like most vampire couples, Oliver and Carmen were seeing each other simply because they knew they looked good together.

"There she is," Jules said, smiling as he got to his feet. "I was beginning to think Teacher kept you after school."

"Thank the Founders it's Thursday!" Lilith laughed as they embraced. "I don't see how clots can stand going to school five days out of the week!" She gave the room a cursory glance as she kissed him on the cheek. "Who's not here yet?"

"Melinda," Carmen replied.

"Big surprise there," Lilith said with a roll of her eyes. "She's *always* late."

"Like you have room to talk! You're not exactly the most punctual," Jules chided.

"Yes, but I'm *fashionably* late, sweetie. There's a difference. So what dish have I missed out on?"

"Ollie was telling us how he managed to score backstage passes to the Victoria's Secret Pink Party for everyone," Carmen said excitedly.

"One of my father's thralls is a publicist for the

company," Oliver explained.

"Victoria's Secret? Oh, please." Lilith sniffed.

"Yeah, I wasn't really sure I wanted to go," Carmen said, her previous enthusiasm suddenly curbed. "What was I thinking?"

"I'm going to get a drink. I need to wash the taste of school out of my mouth," Lilith said. "Don't gossip too much while I'm gone—I'll just make you repeat it when I get back."

As she walked up to the bar made from parts of the church pipe organ, she could see that the bartender was already reaching under the countertop. "The usual?" he asked.

"Of course."

"Here you go," he said, handing her a wineglass filled with something that could be mistaken for claret.

Lilith sniffed the bouquet, smiled, and nodded her approval.

On rejoining her friends, Lilith saw that Melinda had arrived. With her pale jade eyes, café au lait skin, and elaborately braided hair, the daughter of Anton Mauvais was a mesmerizing beauty—and one who was standing a little too close to Jules.

"Glad to see you finally made it, Melly," Lilith said as she slid between the two in such a way that Melinda was forced to take a step back.

"I had to go home to change my clothes," Melinda

explained, "or I would have been here sooner."

"What are you drinking, Lili?" Sergei asked.

"AB neg served at body temperature with a hint of anticoagulant: just the way I like it."

"Yum."

"So—how was school?" Jules prompted.

"Ugh! Please, don't remind me!" Lilith grimaced. "So far we're a week into the fall semester and it already blows donkey dongs."

"I didn't realize that donkey dongs were a unit of measure." Jules chuckled.

"Shut up!" Lilith said, slapping him playfully on the leg. "You know what I mean! Anyway, I was hoping they'd start treating us more like adults and less like fledglings this year. Maybe let us take a field trip, do some luring, you know? No such luck! I can already lure any of the clots in this club with one hand tied behind my back!" She drained her glass and slowly and sensuously licked her lips.

"If that's what you're interested in, we could always go slumming," Tanith suggested. "There are plenty of drug dealers to be found in this city, day or night. No one would notice or care what happened to them."

"Down around Washington Square Park is an easy spot," Jules suggested off-handedly, giving Tanith a wink.

Tanith lifted an eyebrow but was careful to make

sure Lilith didn't see the look on her face. All of Lilith's friends knew better than to respond to Jules's flirting, even in jest.

"Really? So let's go!" Lilith said, refusing to acknowledge Jules's behavior.

The marriage between Lilith Todd and Jules de Laval had been arranged by their families when they were still babies and was viewed as the perfect merger of Old World power and New World wealth.

The de Lavals were the most aristocratic family in the whole city. Jules's father, the Count de Laval, had a bloodright that predated the reign of Clovis I, and he still owned considerable property in his native France.

Despite having changed the family name from Todesking on moving to America, the Todds had no claim to royalty. However, they *were* richer than Midas. By arranging a marriage contract with the de Lavals, Lilith's father had guaranteed that his precious daughter would indeed grow up to be a real princess—or at least a countess—and the de Lavals were assured of the steady stream of money necessary to make sure their collection of châteaus, palaces, and castles remained in the family.

Of course, none of this stopped Jules's eyes—and other body parts—from wandering on a regular basis.

"We could do it this weekend, I guess." He shrugged.

"That's if you don't mind some of the boys tagging along."

"I'm *always* interested in partying," she said, snuggling up to him.

There was a buzzing sound and Jules pulled out his cell phone. "It's my dad," he said with a frown. "I better go."

Lilith tried to angle her head so she could see the name on Jules's caller ID, but he had already palmed the phone. "Since when do you go scampering home when Daddy calls?" she asked.

"Since I got a failing grade on my last alchemy test," Jules replied sourly. "He threatened to cancel my trip to Vail if I didn't put in at least a couple hours studying after school."

"See you tomorrow night, then?"

"Sure," Jules replied. As he bent down to kiss her good-bye, Lilith rose to meet him. Jules cradled the back of her head in his palm as his tongue slipped into her eager, hungry mouth. After a long, final kiss that felt real, he looked into her eyes and gave her his patented sexy smile. "I gotta go, babe. Call me when you get up."

Lilith watched as Jules left. Even though the Loft was packed, the crowd parted without him having to say a word. She silently wondered if he really was going home or if it was simply an excuse to be with someone else. There would be plenty of time for him to go out without her after they got married. Until then, she wanted Jules all to herself. The idea of Jules doing the things to another girl that he did to her was enough to trigger bouts of jealous anxiety in her.

Lilith glanced down at her hands and saw that they were knotted into fists. "Excuse me for a moment, will you?" she said to the others as she stood up. "I need to make a run to the little girls' room."

The VIP lounge's ladies' room was considerably smaller than its counterpart downstairs, with only two toilets and no mirrors mounted on the wall over the sink. Lilith quickly scanned the floor, checking to make sure there weren't any feet visible under the stalls. Satisfied that she was alone, she dropped the lid onto one of the toilets so she could sit down. Her hands were already starting to shake as she pushed the bolt lock home behind her.

She put her Prada bag down between her feet and reached inside, her fingers blindly groping for the zippered pocket where she kept the forbidden stash no one knew about: not her parents, not Tanith, not even Jules.

She just needed a little hit, that's all. Just a little something to take the edge off and boost her self-confidence. Everybody thought she had it so easy. But being the perfect daughter, the perfect friend, the perfect student, the perfect girlfriend all the time was hard work.

She deserved this.

She opened her hand to reveal a small tortoiseshell case compact. She smiled to herself as she unsnapped the compact's lid, revealing its contents.

A small, circular mirror.

Lilith stared at her reflection for a long moment, tilting the compact first one way, then another in order to see as much of her face as possible.

She had been told all her life that she was beautiful. Her mother said so. Her father said so. Jules said so. Tanith said so. And when she became older, others said so—not with words, but with their eyes. Even though she was only sixteen, Lilith was accustomed to lustful looks directed at her by people of all ages and persuasions. Still, no matter how many times others told her she was attractive, it wasn't the same as being able to see it with her own eyes.

However, the relief the small mirror provided her didn't come without a price. If she was ever caught with it in her possession, she would be automatically expelled from school and brought as a criminal before the Synod, the governing counsel that saw to it that the ancient laws of her people were obeyed.

Lilith scrutinized her hair and makeup, checking to make sure she looked her best before clicking the compact shut. As she returned the mirror to its secret hiding place, her hands were once again steady, her manner assured. Before she exited the stall, she made certain to flush the toilet, just in case someone had entered the restroom in the meantime and might be paying attention. After all, appearance was everything.

She was herself again: Lilith Todd, Vampire American Princess.

"Where've you been for so long?" Melinda asked as Lilith rejoined the group.

"I'm bored. You want to go downstairs?" Lilith said, ignoring the question as she drained the last of her drink.

"Sure." Tanith shrugged. "Sergei hates dancing, don't you?"

"All my best moves are in the boudoir." Sergei grinned crookedly. "I'll stay here and catch a buzz, if you don't mind."

"Same here," Oliver said as he sipped his drink.

"Come on," Lilith said, taking Tanith by the hand. "Let's dance." She turned to look at Carmen and Melinda. "Coming?"

Carmen and Melinda exchanged a look, then hopped to their feet and followed their friends without saying a word.

Even though the dance floor was packed, Lilith and her entourage effortlessly moved through the crowd until they reached its center. As the quartet danced, laughed, and giggled among themselves, Lilith became aware that she was being watched. She looked around and saw a man in his mid-thirties staring at her intently.

Normally she ignored the clots that frequented the Belfry, but she was bored and she'd been drinking, and she liked his look. Perhaps she would have a little fun of her own. She met the man's eyes and nodded ever so slightly.

The clot flashed a smile that revealed expensive dental work and moved toward her. She glided up to meet him, her eyes locking onto and holding his own.

On seeing what Lilith was doing, Tanith, Carmen, and Melly quickly positioned themselves between the couple and the surrounding club-goers, effectively isolating the prey from the rest of the humans. As they continued to dance, the clot appeared oblivious to the fact that his newfound partner was gradually working him to the edge of the dance floor.

He placed his hands on Lilith's waist, his eyes blazing with a mixture of lust and pharmaceutically fed heat, but she easily slipped from between his fingers. She smiled, wagging a finger in mock reproach, but still didn't say a word. Instead, she nodded in the direction of the nearby ladies' room. His eyes brightened even more.

After checking to make sure the coast was clear, Lilith quickly led her prey into the restroom, the members of her entourage closing in tight behind her. Tanith followed immediately after her to serve as goalie, while Carmen and Melinda stood guard at the door, turning away possible intruders.

Lilith kept her eyes focused on her prey as she steered him backward, toward the middle toilet stall, the door of which was already standing open.

"So, uh, is your friend interested too?" the clot asked eagerly, his eyes flicking toward Tanith, who stood behind Lilith, blocking his exit to the door.

Lilith glanced over her shoulder at Tanith and the two shared a knowing smile. "Yeah, she'd like a piece of you as well."

Lilith gently pushed her prey farther into the stall until the back of his legs made contact with the porcelain bowl. "In fact, we'd *all* like a little taste of you."

The man grinned as he loosened his tie and dropped down onto the toilet, staring up at Lilith like he had just walked into a hot sex fantasy. Four gorgeous young chicks ready, willing, and able to have group sex with him? What's not to like?

That question was answered when Lilith lunged forward, unsheathing a pair of retractable two-inch fangs, which she buried in his exposed jugular. The clot barely had time for a short, strangled cry of alarm before the neurotoxins in her saliva spread through his system, paralyzing his vocal cords and robbing him of his motor skills. His eyes rolled back in their sockets, showing only whites.

Although she had consumed human blood all her life, Lilith had only experienced the real thing straight from the vein two or three times before. As her prey's blood flooded her mouth, she was amazed at how *alive* it tasted. She sucked greedily at the crimson liquid, shivering in delight as her prey's vitality spread throughout her body.

"Hey, don't bogart him." Tanith grinned as she tapped Lilith on the shoulder.

"Be my guest," Lilith said as she stepped aside to give her friend a turn.

Tanith picked up the clot's limp right arm, pushing the sleeve of his suit back as she bit into his exposed wrist. He didn't moan or even blink.

As Lilith looked away from the scene in the bathroom stall, her attention was caught by her reflection in the mirror above the washbasins. She moved closer, transfixed by the sight of her mouth glistening red and wet, as if coated in fresh lipstick. Behind her she could see Tanith emerging from the stall, blotting her lips on a piece of toilet paper, as Carmen ducked in for her share of the evening's fun.

Suddenly there was a flurry of noise as Sebastian

pushed his way into the ladies' room. He had a wireless headset clipped to one ear and a concerned look on his face.

"What in the name of hell is going on here? I got a report that someone was blocking access to the women's restroom."

Lilith moved to put herself between the club promoter and the toilets. "It's just girl stuff, you know. Nothing to get upset over, Seb."

"What are you kids doing downstairs anyway—? Is the ladies' room in the VIP lounge not working?" Sebastian's gaze dropped to the floor and his eyes widened. "Wait a minute—are those *men's* shoes?"

Stepping around Lilith, he yanked open the door of the stall and stared at the man propped up on the toilet like an oversize rag doll. The clot's chin rested on his breastbone and his skin was nearly as white as the surrounding tile. Sebastian grabbed the man by the hair and lifted his head, then let it drop.

"What have you *done?*" he yelped. "You know the rules—no tapping on the premises! At least not during club hours!"

"Look, Seb—don't get upset, okay?" Lilith said, trying to defuse the promoter's alarm. "You can always put him in the cellar with the others, right?"

"Don't get *upset?*" Sebastian growled, flashing his fangs in open annoyance. "Do you *know* who this is?"

Lilith and the others looked among themselves and shook their heads. During the thrill of the hunt, no one had bothered to ask the prey his name.

"This man is a *very important* music industry executive! He can't just *disappear*! And he most certainly can't disappear from *my* club!" Sebastian picked up the clot's limp right arm and felt his wrist. "He's still alive. Praise the Founders for small favors."

"Maybe we can drop him off at a hospital or something?" Tanith suggested.

"He's *not* going to an emergency room with all those bites on him!" Sebastian snarled, clearly irritated by the huge inconvenience of it all. "He looks like he fell into a snake pit." Sebastian pressed a finger to his Bluetooth and shouted angrily into the mouthpiece. "Andre! I want the ladies' room in the chapel sealed off *immediately*! See to it no one, and I mean *no one*, comes in here. I dunno—tell 'em someone flushed a sanitary napkin."

"So what do we do now?" Lilith asked. She had never seen Sebastian so angry before and it made her uncomfortable.

Sebastian heaved a sigh and rubbed his furrowed brow with the heel of his palm, doing his best to reel his temper in. "What's done is done. I'll handle this. There's no point in freaking out, okay? I'll take care of our friend here. I'll have the boys run a transfusion on him. He'll wake up sick as a dog. Knowing this prick, he'll just assume he got lucky. But you're going to have to leave and stay away for a while."

"You mean we're *banned* from the club?" Tanith wailed.

"Oh, c'mon, Seb—aren't you overreacting?" Melinda asked.

"Overreacting?" Sebastian barked, rolling his eyes in disgust. "We can't run the risk of attracting attention here! Police would be bad enough, but the last thing the Belfry needs is Van Helsings!"

"But if we're banned from here, where will we party this weekend?" Carmen pouted.

"Anywhere but here," Sebastian growled. "For all I care, you can party in hell."

CHAPTER 2

Lilith groaned aloud as she huddled under her 980-thread Egyptian cotton sheets. Perhaps tapping that cokehead's vein hadn't been such a good idea after all. Although she was practically immortal and immune to virtually all human illnesses, drinking drug-laced blood could still bring a hangover.

She rolled over and squinted at the alarm clock next to her bed. According to the numbers it was three in the afternoon. She had promised to hook up with Tanith before five and do some shopping. Although she normally disliked going out before sunset, Lilith was willing to make the occasional sacrifice if it meant hitting Prada or Tiffany while they were still open.

She stretched her lithe, lean body, savoring the feel of the twelve-hundred-dollar sheets against her skin.

Sitting up, she punched the call button on the intercom next to her alarm clock.

"Yes, Miss Lilith?" a male voice promptly responded.

"I'm awake, Curtis," she said. "Send my dresser up."

"Right away, Miss Lilith."

Lilith threw back the covers and swung her legs over the edge of the bed, which had been in her family since the days of Louis XV. She had long since learned how to physically dress herself, but she still needed her dresser, Esmeralda, to help her with her hair and makeup and always would.

Before she went into her bathroom, she double-checked to make sure all the curtains in the bedroom were pulled tight against the afternoon sun. Although she could walk around during the daylight hours without any adverse side effects, the same could not be said of the undead who served her family. The last thing she needed was her dresser bursting into flame just before she left to go shopping.

Satisfied that the room was adequately sun-proofed, she headed into her bathroom, which had separate chambers for her facial chair and tanning bed.

While she waited for the shower water to heat up, Lilith shucked off her silk chiffon cami-doll and punted it into the corner of the room. She luxuriated in the feel of the water pulsing against her skin as she lathered up with a body wash made for her by the family's private perfumier.

There was a light tap on the door as she stepped out of the shower. "Are you ready for me, Miss Lilith?" the dresser asked, pushing open the bathroom door wide enough to stick her head inside.

Esmeralda looked to be in her early thirties, with an olive complexion, raven-black eyes, and long, thick dark hair pulled back into a simple ponytail fixed with golden bangles. Lilith had never asked her, but she figured the dresser must have been a gypsy before she became one of the undead.

"Go ahead and set up, Ezzie," Lilith replied. "I'm going to get dressed."

"As you wish, Miss Lilith," the dresser said, stepping aside to allow her mistress to pass before entering the bathroom, her black-and-chrome makeup case trundling along behind her like a pet on wheels.

Lilith darted across the room and opened the door of her walk-in closet. She snatched a pair of quartz-pink silk Perla briefs and a matching underwire from the top drawer of the antique cherrywood lingerie chest. She looked with distaste at her school uniforms, which were hanging in their own section of the closet, as if they might somehow contaminate the rest of her belongings. After fifteen minutes she finally decided on a pink Marc Jacobs blouse and a Chloé skirt, with flowered wedges. Maybe she'd buy something new to wear tonight.

She reentered the bathroom just as Esmeralda was

placing her last set of makeup brushes on a crisp, clean towel. The dresser's cosmetic case stood open, unfolded like some kind of exotic night-blooming flower, revealing the countless jars, tubes, sticks, and trays necessary to her profession.

As Lilith hopped into the leather facial chair, her eyes automatically went to the blank space where her vanity mirror would have been if she was like every other girl in her apartment building.

"Why can't I have just one mirror, Ezzie?"

"You know they're forbidden, Miss Lilith," Esmeralda replied wearily as she busied herself with putting Sisley foundation makeup on her mistress's face.

"I know, but it's not fair. *I* still reflect. Just because everyone *else* around here is too old to look into mirrors doesn't mean *I* have to be punished as well."

"True, you still cast a reflection," Esmeralda said as she continued to apply the cosmetics. "But not for much longer. Once you fully mature from fledgling to adult, you will no longer reflect. You know it is against the decree of the Synod to own mirrors."

Realizing there was no way to get around that particular argument, Lilith decided to shift the conversation. "Did you look at those magazines I gave you?"

"Yes, I looked at them." The dresser sighed.

At one time Esmeralda had served as the personal beautician for some old French king's slutty girlfriend, and it was clear she resented having the latest Italian

Vogue and *W* shoved under her nose all the time. It wasn't that Lilith thought Esmeralda did a bad job; she just wanted to look hot, that was all. One of the things they'd taught at school, which she had to admit was actually useful, was that it was important to stay abreast of the current fashion trends and not get stuck with a certain "look." If she wasn't careful, she could find herself looking like Carmen's mother, who still dressed like a 1940s film star.

"Do you think you can make me look more like her?" Lilith asked, pointing at a picture of a glamorous young celebrity walking down yet another red carpet.

Esmeralda gave Lilith a deliciously evil smile. "*Feh!* I can make it seem that *she* looks like *you*."

Lilith wanted to giggle, but she knew she had to remain absolutely still so Esmeralda could finish her work. After all, it was important that she go out into the world looking more human than the humans.

"Good afternoon, Miss Todd," the doorman said as he held the brass-plated door to the Balmoral open for Lilith. "You're out and about early today, I see."

Lilith nodded to acknowledge the human thrall's comment, but she didn't dignify him with a reply. Although most of the other tenants who shared their Park Avenue apartment building had no clue about the true nature of the penthouse's residents, everyone on the building's staff was under her father's control.

The Rolls was there, as usual. The daylight driver was on duty, waiting to take Lilith wherever she might want to go. He touched the bill of his cap respectfully as he let her into the limo.

Once comfortable, Lilith began digging through her purse in search of her iPhone. There were a couple of text messages already waiting for her as she powered it up.

The first was from Tanith, asking if Lilith was as hungover as she was; the second was from Carmen, who wanted to know if she was still going to Dolce & Gabbana. She quickly texted *yes* back to both, then hit the speed dial, counting the number of rings on the other end. Jules picked up on the third.

"I was wondering when you'd call," he said with a sleepy laugh. "I was beginning to think Van Helsings caught you on the way home."

"No such luck!" Lilith laughed. "Did I wake you up?"

"Not really," he replied, stifling a yawn. "I'm just taking my time getting out of bed."

"Alone, I trust."

"You wanna hook up at the Belfry later?" he suggested.

Lilith tried not to notice that Jules didn't return her laugh or acknowledge her comment about someone else being in his bed.

They'd gone through more than one argument about

her jealousy. The last time they had a fight, he told her if she accused him of cheating on her again, he'd go ahead and do it for real.

Instead she replied, "It's a bit of a long story, but we've been temporarily banned from the club."

"*What?!?*" Suddenly Jules no longer sounded the least bit sleepy. "Lilith," he teased, "did you do something wicked?"

"It's nothing, really. Seb just got his panties in a twist. You know how he is. In a couple of days all will be forgiven."

"Yeah, but until then where do we go to party?"

"Why don't we go slumming in the Village?"

"I guess we could do that."

"Hey, we're here! Gotta go! See you later?"

"Later."

Lilith snapped her phone shut as the Rolls came to a halt outside the D&G boutique at Madison and Sixty-ninth. She made sure her oversize bug-eyed Fendi sunglasses were firmly in place before she climbed out of the limo. Although she could walk around during the day without fear of turning into a piece of beef jerky, the direct sunlight was still painful to her eyes.

"I'll page you when I'm ready to go," she told the daylight driver.

Lilith loved going to Dolce & Gabbana. Everything about the place, from the crystal doorknob to the gold ceiling fixtures to the pillows adorning the couches in the fitting room, was extravagant. Plus the fashions were a much-needed break from those dreadful uniforms she was forced to wear to school.

As Lilith entered the boutique, a couple of shoppers on the floor stopped to stare at her, then began to excitedly whisper back and forth behind their hands. From the looks on their faces Lilith realized they had mistaken her for one of the glittery divas the designers were so popular with.

As she browsed the fragrance counter, Lilith noticed a bearded man in his thirties standing off to the side, openly watching her. Although she was accustomed to being ogled by older men, there was something different in the way he was staring at her.

Lilith turned to meet the stranger's gaze. "Why don't you take a picture?" she quipped. "It'll last longer."

Unlike most of the dirty old men she caught drooling over her, he didn't hastily look away, but instead smiled at her. "Perhaps I will, someday," he said, placing a business card facedown on the glass countertop as he walked out of the shop. "Enjoy your shopping, my dear."

Lilith picked up the card and flipped it over. Printed on the other side in raised letters were the words KRISTOF: PHOTOGRAPHER, along with a phone number. With a flash of excitement, she slipped it into her purse.

"Lili!"

Lilith looked up and saw Tanith walking toward

her across the store's highly polished mosaic floor. Her friend was dressed in a cherry-red Gucci dress, silver wedges, and a pair of Prada sunglasses.

"I was starting to wonder if you'd forgotten me!" Tanith said as they clasped hands and air-kissed.

"Like that could ever happen!" Lilith chuckled as she slipped her arm through her friend's elbow. "So—have you had a chance to pick out anything yet?"

"I've got a lavender dress set aside, but I want you there when I try it on. Oh, and I saw this peacock-blue cocktail dress that would look *perfect* on you! It's super-short."

"What would I do without you looking out for me?" Lilith sighed.

"Hey, that's what friends are for, right?" Tanith replied.

"It seems weird that in a few years we won't be able to do this anymore," Lilith said wistfully.

"What? Go shopping together?" Tanith frowned.

"No," Lilith replied. "I mean this." She tapped the dressing room mirror, being careful not to accidentally damage its surface. Like all vampires, Lilith's neatly painted nails were exceptionally hard, like talons. "By the time we're twenty-five, we won't be able to see our reflections. And neither will anyone else! That means no more shopping in places like this, you know."

"Yeah, it's a bummer," Tanith admitted. "But try

not to think about it. There's no point in dwelling on things you can't change. I rarely look at mirrors as it is. Besides, there are always shops like Sister Midnight's. Still, you know what they say—use it before you lose it!" She laughed.

"Yeah, I guess you're right." Lilith smiled weakly.

Tanith gave her friend a curious look. "You seem a bit low, Lili. Things okay with you and Jules?"

"They're good," Lilith replied with a dismissive wave of her hand. "I'm still feeling the effects of last night, I guess."

"I *know*! What was that guy on?" Tanith shook her head.

"Anyway, you and Sergei seem to be into it."

"He's fun, but we're just fooling around. He's promised to some girl back in the Old Country that he's never met. He's *very* sexy, though." Tanith wiggled into the lavender shredded silk cocktail dress. "How does it look?"

"That color really suits you," Lilith said, stepping out of her own clothes and slipping into the blue dress. "I didn't realize Sergei was already promised. Too bad. You make a cute couple." She ran her hands across her taut belly and over her hips as she turned first one way, then another, admiring how the low, tight-cut neckline highlighted her cleavage. "You were right: I *do* look perfect in this dress."

"All you need is a pair of sexy shoes and you'll be set,"

Tanith said. "You know, Lili, you're pretty lucky—you and Jules actually have a chance to get to know each other before you're bound. For all Sergei knows, the girl he's promised to could look like an Orlock."

Lilith burst out laughing despite herself and quickly clapped her hands over her mouth. "You shouldn't say things like that, Tanith!" she said in mock reproach. "You *know* Exo is Jules's cousin!"

Xander Orlock, known as Exo to his friends and family, was Jules's first cousin. Exo's mother was Jules's father's beautiful younger sister, Juliana, who was the second wife of Count Boris Orlock, patriarch of one of the oldest and most powerful families in the world. The Orlocks were infamous for inbreeding to keep their bloodright, which went back to Urlok, one of the thirteen Founders, undiluted.

Having Juliana marry into the Orlocks had been a real coup for the de Lavals, even though all that inbreeding had resulted in the count being freakishly ugly.

"Exo's not that bad-looking, in a Mr. Spock kinda way, I guess," Tanith said with a shrug. "I was thinking more along the lines of his dad or that older brother of his."

"*Brrr!*" Lilith feigned a shudder. "Don't bring *him* up! Just thinking about Klaus creeps me out. I'm glad that the Orlocks are only going to be related to me by marriage, not blood."

As they returned to prowl the boutique's racks for

more clothes, Lilith saw Melinda walking toward them with Carmen in tow.

"Let's shop!"

It was a half hour after closing by the time the quartet finished picking and choosing, their platinum credit cards guaranteeing the store manager's willingness to hang around to lock up after them. The setting sun glinted off their custom gold foil shopping bags as they gathered on the sidewalk in front of the boutique.

"What next?" Melinda asked.

"We could go back to my place for a few drinks," Tanith suggested. "My parents are leaving for Brazil tonight."

"That's a great idea!" Lilith grinned.

Melinda said, "Why don't we walk?"

"Sounds good to me," Lilith agreed. "I'll send my driver home and call Jules so he and the boys will know to hook up with us at Tanith's. We can double up and take a couple of cars to the Village. This is going to be fun!"

The girls chatted among themselves as they strolled in the gathering twilight. As the quartet moved past the opulent stores along Madison Avenue, every head turned to watch them go by. Lilith and her friends pretended not to notice the attention. Some of the humans out walking that evening stared because they thought the four incredibly beautiful, expensively dressed young women were fashion models or Hollywood starlets. Others stared out of lust. But a handful stared because they sensed the truth behind the mask and were unable to look away, like birds hypnotized by the sway of the cobra's dance.

When Tanith was a little girl, she used to tell people that she lived across the street from the Alice in Wonderland statue in Central Park. Now she preferred to give Jimmy Choo's as a reference point. Hardly glancing at the fabulous shoes in the window, the friends turned down Sixty-third to Fifth Avenue.

Three undead servants were standing in the hallway, loaded down with luggage, when the elevator opened on Tanith's penthouse floor. As the girls stepped off, the servants filed onto the waiting elevator without saying a word.

"Damn it!" Tanith groaned. "They're still here!"

"Not for much longer," her father said dryly as he exited their apartment. With his wavy dark hair and heavily lidded eyes, Dorian Graves looked like he had just walked off the cover of a gothic romance novel. He gave Tanith a peck on the cheek. "Be a good girl and promise not to burn the house to the ground while we're gone, will you?"

"Only if you promise to bring me back something sparkly."

"Don't I always?" He chuckled. "Well, I'm afraid I

must be going. Your mother is already downstairs. We'll be back late next week. So long, young ladies," he said, acknowledging his daughter's friends with a gentlemanly nod as he stepped inside the elevator.

"Well, that's over with," Tanith said with a sigh of relief as the elevator doors shut behind her father. "Feel free to make yourselves comfortable."

"Don't mind if I do." Lilith grinned as she tossed her shopping bags on the floor, shucked off her heels, and wiggled her pedicured toes in the plush carpet. Tanith made her way to the formal bar in the corner, where her father kept the good stuff. She opened up the refrigerator and took out a bag of A neg laced with Napoleon brandy while Carmen and Melly kicked back on the leather sofa. Tanith poured the blood into four crystal snifters and handed them out to her friends.

"To us," Lilith said, holding her glass merrily aloft.

"To us," Tanith, Carmen, and Melinda echoed, lifting their glasses in a toast.

"To the vampire princesses of New York City! Long may we reign!"

CHAPTER 3

"So, where are we slumming tonight?" Melinda asked as she bounced a quarter off the coffee table, narrowly missing the Waterford Crystal juice glass set at its center.

"Washington Square Park," Jules explained as he tossed the coin with an expert flip of his fingers, bouncing it into the empty glass. "All right!" He grinned. He studied the others for a long moment, as if it was a matter of life or death, before pointing at Lilith. "Lili has to take a shot."

"Like you'd have to twist my arm otherwise." Lilith laughed as she picked up the shot of tequila-laced O poz. "Here's blood in your eye," she said, knocking back the drink with a toss of her head.

"Okay, since I made the bounce that time, I get to go again," Jules said, taking the coin back out of the glass.

"How much longer before we can leave?" Lilith asked, getting bored. After last night, she was eager to be on the hunt.

Jules paused to glance at his watch. "I guess it's late enough. We could leave now, since it'll take a little while to get down there. I know a new club we can hit later."

"Cool. I'll tell Tanith." Lilith strolled over to Tanith and Sergei, who lay sprawled on the carpet making out. She gave Tanith's hip a playful nudge with her bare foot. "C'mon, you two, give it a rest! It's time this party hit the streets."

Reluctantly Tanith pulled away from Sergei and smiled up at Lilith with hazy eyes. "I'm just getting warmed up."

"Do you think we'll be safe?" Sergei asked.

"Are you still obsessing about Van Helsings?" Lilith chuckled. "It's just a bogeyman story the adults use to try and scare us from having fun."

"I don't know about that . . . my grandfather was killed by Van Helsings," Sergei said.

"What's the matter, Sergei?" Tanith purred. "Afraid the big, bad vampire hunters are gonna get you too? C'mon—that happened, what? Seventy-five? A hundred years ago?"

"One hundred and twenty," he admitted.

"See? It's old news!" Lilith insisted. "When's the last

"Have you ever tangled with a New Blood, Lilith?" Oliver asked.

"No," she replied. "Unless you want to count the Maledetto twins."

"That's not fair," Melinda said. "Bella and Bette's dad might be a newbie, but their mother's bloodright goes all the way back to Aeneas."

"Yeah, but only one of them is going to inherit it," Carmen replied.

"Hey, we can take them on," Jules said, tired of all the procrastination.

Lilith picked up his cue. "I'm up for tapping some fresh red. Who's with me on that?" She grinned as her friends raised their voices in a raucous cheer.

"That's what I thought."

Every vampire is taught from childhood that the easiest prey is the common prostitute or drug dealer. Such humans are used to being approached by strangers. They're willing to go to secluded areas with little persuasion. And when one of them disappears, who cares? True, sometimes individuals with specialized skills are needed, but the vast majority of undead who serve the true-born were once nothing more than criminals, whores, addicts, and pushers.

This was why, with all of Manhattan to choose from, Lilith and her friends were taking Jules's Mercedes and Tanith's Bentley to Washington Square Park in search of kicks.

"My father would spit blood if he knew I was out slumming." Lilith laughed. "I'm such a naughty girl."

"Naughty, yes—but also nice." Jules chuckled as he slid a hand up her skirt, caressing her upper thigh.

"I *love* slumming, don't you?" Lilith purred as she leaned her head against Jules's shoulder, shifting to allow his hand easier access. "It's so exciting. Luring a real, live victim gets me hot."

"Me too," Jules agreed as he fingered the elastic of her Agent Provocateur thong.

"Not now, Jules," Lilith said as she slithered free of his grasp. "Later. After the hunt."

Jules's eyes flashed as if he might press the issue, then he smiled and withdrew his hand from between her legs. "Whatever you say, baby."

Lilith looked out the windows and saw that the Mercedes had come to a stop and that they were parked a few blocks from their destination. "We're here!" she shouted triumphantly, reaching over and popping open the door before the driver could do it for her. She looked over her shoulder and saw the others climbing out of Tanith's Bentley.

"Catch me if you can!" Lilith whooped, laughing as her friends chased after her, their shouts and laughter echoing through the narrow, angled streets of Greenwich Village.

Although it was after two in the morning, the streets were far from deserted. There were still plenty of younger people, coming and going from various clubs and all-night diners, laughing and joking. As far as the casual observer could tell, Lilith and her friends were just another boisterous group of college kids on their way back to the NYU dorms after a night of partying.

Still giggling among themselves, the group headed toward the triumphal arch at the foot of Fifth Avenue and Washington Square North. Dramatically lit by strategically placed spotlights, the white marble monument looked like a giant gravestone.

Although lampposts lined the pathways, the park itself was considerably darker than the surrounding neighborhood. As the vampires walked through the arch to the large recessed fountain basin in the center of the square, they could make out at least a half dozen men prowling near the metal benches that ringed the path around the fountain wall. These shadowy figures in baggy pants, running shoes, and hooded sweatshirts were the true lords of Washington Square Park.

No doubt the dealers also thought Lilith and her friends were just another group of drunken revelers in search of drugs. Lilith smiled in anticipation of the look of terrified surprise on the prey's face when he finally realized the truth.

Jules motioned for them to gather in closer, taking cover behind a small cluster of trees and a low fence with a sign that read STAY OFF THE GRASS. As usual, he had to play the role of the game master, setting down the rules for the others.

"One of us goes in and trances the prey into following them somewhere secluded, then we all move in. Extra points for trophies—something personal—from the prey. Drugs don't count. Now that we've got the ground rules, who wants to play the bait?"

"Ooh! Ooh! Me!" Lilith said, waving her arm as if she were begging the teacher to call on her in class.

"Very well, Lilith it is," he said with a laugh.

She turned and peered out from between the trees at the men loitering on the west side of the central fountain. She saw a fat African American guy with a gray beard sitting on a bench with an I ♥ New York shopping bag stuffed full of what looked like wadded newspaper and discarded fast-food containers next to him.

Ewww. She wasn't going to put the moves on some old, gross Buddha-belly guy. Whoever she picked had to at least be young and in good shape.

She zeroed in on a tall, gangly dealer leaning against one of the large carved granite outcroppings that were set into the fountain's sit wall like the points of a compass. His face was turned away from her and his hands were hidden in the slash pockets of his navy blue hooded jacket.

The dealer's head swiveled like a radar dish as she approached, giving voice to the ubiquitous cry of the dealer: "Smoke? Smoke?"

Lilith stopped and turned to face him but didn't speak. Reading this as interest from a potential customer, the dealer motioned for her to move closer.

"How many?"

Lilith didn't step closer but instead favored him with a half smile. She saw the look on his face change from one of pure business to one that anticipated, hoped for, pleasure.

"You lookin' for something more, baby? 'Cause whatever it is, I got it," he bragged.

Lilith ached to say something catty, but she didn't dare speak for fear of breaking her concentration. Since the easiest way to control a mind is to have the prey willingly focus on you and look you right in the eyes, being physically attractive is a distinct advantage.

As the dealer stared at the beautiful young girl before him, he suddenly realized he couldn't take his eyes off her. It was as if the entire world had telescoped down to her achingly perfect oval face and eyes, which seemed to glow in the dimness like those of a cat.

Lilith thought, *Come with me,* as hard as she could.

Although his arms and legs were numb, as if someone had shot them full of novocaine, the dealer was seized by the desire to walk with this strange angel, wherever she might lead.

Lilith smiled to herself as he began to move toward her. However, before her prey took a second step, his head suddenly whipped to one side, as if he had heard someone shout his name—and then he stepped back.

What the hell?

Somehow the dealer's mind had slipped free of her control. This was definitely *not* supposed to happen, at least not to *her*. Lilith furrowed her brow, redoubling her concentration.

Look at me.

As the dealer slowly turned his head back toward her, Lilith could see that his eyes were unfocused and his jaw slack: obvious signs that the clot was indeed mesmerized.

Come with me.

The dealer stepped forward yet again, only to suddenly stop and wobble slightly on one foot, like a kid playing a game of freeze tag.

Lilith's face began to burn with frustration. She had no doubt the others were giggling their asses off as they watched her from their hiding place in the shadows.

NOW!

Her command echoed in the dealer's head like feedback from an electric guitar, causing him to lurch forward as if he'd been jabbed with a pitchfork. However, a fraction of a second later he jumped backward, slamming into the granite outcropping so violently it looked like a phantom hand had shoved him against it.

Lilith scowled as she tried to figure out what was going on. The way her prey moved was more like a puppet on a string than an animal trying to escape a snare. But what could cause that kind of interference?

Just as it occurred to Lilith that she might not be the only one inside the dealer's head, a girl she had never seen before stepped out from behind the other side of the outcropping. The stranger was dressed in a pair of gray skinny jeans, purple tweed boots, a long black shirt, and a cropped, faded black leather bomber jacket. Her dark hair was worn in a blunt, jagged bob that, along with her full lips and high cheekbones, made her look like a semi-feral pixie. With a start Lilith realized she was standing face-to-face with a New Blood.

"This one is mine!" the New Blood growled, pointing to the dealer, who stood pinned like a butterfly against the outcropping, drool dripping from his mouth.

"Get lost, skank," Lilith hissed, unsheathing her fangs in ritual challenge. "He belongs to me!"

"*You* get lost, bitch," the New Blood snarled in response, her eyes glowing. "I was here *first*!"

Lilith stepped forward, her hands clenched into fists. "How *dare* you speak to *me* like that! Don't you *know* who I *am*?"

"Yeah," the New Blood sneered. "You're the snooty uptown bitch whose *ass* I'm gonna *kick*!"

The two glared at each other as they circled like boxers getting ready to fight. Lilith took a swipe at her rival, eager to slice the New Blood's clothes and flesh to ribbons with her razor-sharp talons. However, the New Blood proved unexpectedly agile, sidestepping her charge with the grace of a matador. Lilith whirled around, surprised by the other girl's speed.

The New Blood laughed at the startled look on Lilith's face. "You oldies talk a good game, but when it comes down to it, you're nothing but a wuss!" The New Blood's laughter was abruptly replaced by a screech of pain as Lilith drove her nails into her opponent's right side.

"First blood is mine!" Lilith sneered as she yanked her hand free. "So who's the wuss now, newbie?"

The New Blood staggered, her right hand clamping her side, bright red blood oozing from between her fingers. Although her body was already rapidly healing, she would be vulnerable to attack for the next minute— more than enough time for Lilith to deliver the coup de grace. The New Blood's eyes rolled back in their sockets until only the whites were visible.

"What's the matter, newbie?" Lilith taunted. "You're not going to pass out on me, are you?"

If the New Blood had a response to Lilith's jeers, it was lost in the howling wind that suddenly churned every piece of trash in the plaza into a maelstrom of grit and refuse, chasing most of the remaining dealers from the park.

As Lilith raised her arms to shield her face from the stinging lash of the maelstrom, she saw Tanith and Jules running toward her from their hiding place.

Eyes still rolled back in her head, the New Blood raised a hand, as if reaching for an invisible rope, and then closed it into a fist. There was a sound like someone running through dry autumn leaves, and a nimbus of pale blue fire blinked into existence around her clenched fist.

"Lilith!" Tanith shouted over the roar of the wind. *"Get away from her! She's a stormgatherer!"*

Lilith turned to stare at her adversary, who now held a ball of bluish-white lightning in the palm of her hand. Her previous bravado was quickly replaced by fear. Although vampires can resist every human disease and have regenerative powers that make every wound except decapitation or a stake through the heart a matter of inconvenience, electricity can kill them.

As she backed away from the New Blood, Lilith saw Jules running toward her. *"Jules! Help me!"* she yelled.

Lilith's shout broke the New Blood's concentration, causing her eyes to suddenly drop back into their sockets like the reels on a slot machine. Although the gale-force winds instantly died away, she still held a fistful of crackling lightning.

Freed from his trance, the dealer abruptly jerked

awake and fled into the darkness beyond the ring of lights surrounding the plaza. In the next moment the heavyset, bearded dealer seated on the bench jumped to his feet and pulled a compound crossbow out of his shopping bag.

"*Van Helsings!*" Jules shouted in warning.

"*Lilith! Look out!*" Tanith screamed.

As Lilith ran toward her friends, she looked over her shoulder just in time to see the vampire hunter fire his weapon at her. Instinctively she threw herself to one side at the last second, the arrow coming so close it grazed her rib as it flew by. Tanith wasn't as lucky. She hit the ground like a dropped doll, the bolt from the crossbow jutting from her breast.

Lilith fell to her knees beside her friend. "Get up, Tanith! You *have* to get up!"

As the vampire hunter raised his weapon for a second shot, the New Blood flicked her wrist, tossing the lightning ball at him, then turned and fled, disappearing into the shadows without looking back.

There was a horrific scream, followed by the smell of burning flesh and hair, as the fistful of lightning struck the vampire hunter square in the chest. He dropped his crossbow and fell to the ground in a twitching heap.

Jules stood over Lilith as she knelt beside Tanith's body, frantically scanning the area for signs of more Van Helsings. Although he had never gone up against them before, he knew the vampire hunters didn't travel alone. Sure enough, he spotted three more, dressed like drug dealers, running toward them from the other side of the park, each armed with a crossbow.

"It's an ambush!" Jules shouted as he yanked Lilith to her feet. "Forget about Tanith—she's dead! We've got to get out of—!" Before he could finish his sentence, the closest of the advancing Van Helsings fired on him. The young vampire roared in pain and leaped at his attackers, fangs and claws bared.

The Van Helsing instinctively fell back, screaming as a monster with the wings of a bat and the face of a man swooped toward him, an arrow in its thigh.

Jules grabbed the vampire hunter's crossbow with his clawlike feet, yanking it and its owner into the air.

"Shoot it!" the Van Helsing yelled as he struggled to free himself from Jules's clutches. "Don't worry about hitting me! Just shoot!"

Jules banked sharply and let go of his unwilling passenger, sending the Van Helsing flying into a park bench. As the other vampire hunters hurried to their comrade's aid, Jules soared into the night, leaving Lilith to escape the best she could.

"Damn it, the stormgatherer got away," Drummer growled as he got to his feet.

"Are you okay?"

"I'll live." His right arm felt like it had been wrenched from its socket, and he was pretty sure he had at least one cracked rib, but all things considered, he was in fairly decent shape. He waved the others away with a pained grimace. "Don't worry about me—go see to Big Ike."

Rémy, the older of the two, hurried over to the big man's body and checked his pulse. "He's badly burned—especially his hands—but he's still alive. Lucky for him he was wearing rubber-soled shoes."

"Get on the horn to removal," Drummer grunted. "Tell them we have a man down."

"What about her?" Kevin pointed at the body of the vampiress sprawled across the pavement.

"You know the drill," Drummer replied. "Suckers like to play possum. We have to make sure she's dead."

"Gotcha," Kevin replied as he pulled his Ghurka knife from its sheath and cautiously nudged the body with his boot. "You know, I've never seen a sucker summon up a tornado before—or turn into a bat, or whatever that thing was."

"That's because up to now, you've only taken down undead," Drummer explained. "Undead can't shape-shift or control the weather. What we went up against tonight were true-borns. Old Bloods, most likely." He frowned as he stared down at the dead girl. The vampiress looked disconcertingly young and pretty—no more than sixteen or seventeen. He scratched his head in confusion. "That's funny; I could have *sworn* the blonde was wearing blue. . . ."

"You mean like this?" Rémy asked, holding up the shredded remains of a peacock-blue silk dress.

"Where did you find that?" Drummer asked suspiciously.

"It was lying over there, right next to the fountain." Before Rémy could turn to point out where he had found the ruined garment, he heard a deep, guttural growl that stopped him in his tracks.

Suddenly a huge wolf with piercing blue eyes and no tail leaped out of the fountain basin in an explosive spray of cold water, knocking Rémy to the ground.

"Shoot her!" Drummer yelled, firing his crossbow at the fleeing creature. "She's getting away!" His arrow fell short, bouncing harmlessly against the pavement as the monster wolf disappeared into the streets.

"Damn it!" Drummer snapped, hurling the crossbow to the ground despite the excruciating pain in his shoulder. "The boss is going to lose it when he hears about this!"

CHAPTER 4

Cally Monture shook her head in disgust as she hurried down the stairs to the subway. What was she thinking? She should have let the bimbo in the awful blue dress take the prey. But no, she let her pride get in the way, and now she was running for her life. Granny had warned her about letting her temper get the better of her in tight situations and, as always, had been proven right. Cally was relieved the old woman was no longer around to see how badly she had screwed up—but only a little, for she sorely missed her grandmother.

Although she had been stalking the park off and on for several months, this was the first time she had run into real problems. She probably would have rethought her plans for the night if she'd known she would be crossing paths not only with Old Bloods, but Van Helsings as well.

Given the Van Helsings' reputation for zealotry and the Old Bloods' tendency for vindictiveness, both were extremely dangerous foes. Cally was glad her grandmother had finally relented and taught her a couple of spells before she died. At least she could defend herself, to a certain extent. Still, she'd been extremely lucky that the Old Bloods were fledglings like herself. Had they been adults, she probably would have been killed, stormgatherer or not.

As she strode toward the stairs leading to the platforms, she looked around for signs of pursuit. Since Van Helsings and vampires never liked to call attention to themselves in public places, she was probably safe as long as she made sure there were plenty of witnesses nearby.

As she leaned out from the platform in hopes of spotting the next outbound, she noticed a hot guy in fashionably distressed skinny jeans and a denim jacket waiting for the train. He was buff, judging by the fit of his vintage T-shirt. He was pretending to read a paperback, but Cally could tell he was secretly checking her out.

He was clean-shaven with a large, expressive mouth, dark brown eyes, and wavy, reddish-brown hair. Although he looked to be about eighteen or nineteen, he exuded the kind of serious, mature vibe Cally usually associated with dudes in their twenties. Maybe he was just emo.

When he glanced up from his reading yet again, Cally met his gaze. As their eyes locked, she felt a slight tingling inside her, not unlike the one she got as she called down lightning. For the briefest of heartbeats, it was as if the air between them crackled with energy. She flashed the handsome stranger a smile, only to have him blush and bury his nose in his paperback. Yeah, definitely emo.

At any other time she would have flirted with him—at least a little—but when the tunnel lights switched from red to green, Cally quickly forgot about her admirer. As her train pulled in, she slipped inside and stood near the door. There were a handful of commuters in the car with her, mostly partyers headed home after a long night at the clubs.

When she got off the train a couple of stops later, she thought she saw the guy in skinny jeans getting out onto the platform one car down from her. She turned around to make sure, but no one was there. She put him out of her mind and hurried down the passageway to her next train.

Now that she had enough space between herself and her potential enemies, Cally took the time to quickly count her earnings for the night. She was disappointed to find she had barely two hundred dollars. Normally she could score at least twice that off the dealers in the park. She frowned in dismay as she tucked the bills back inside her bra.

She needed cash for the next emergency. And she didn't need a fortune-teller to know there'd be one.

Although her father sent money on a regular basis, her mother had a way of blowing it all on things she "had" to have, like a giant flat-screen TV or a two-day spa treatment. So paying the electric bill or the mortgage on the condo often fell to Cally. Cally wondered for a moment what might become of her mother if she had been the one to catch the crossbow bolt earlier, but the thought was so distressing she instantly blocked it from her mind.

There's no point in worrying about things that haven't happened, she told herself. *Focus on getting back home; that's all that matters. Just one more train, and I'm home free.*

There was the sound of a shoe scuffing against concrete behind her. Cally turned to see the figure of a man headed down the stairs from the concourse above. Panic rose in her like floodwater as she looked around the platform and realized that she was totally alone.

She ducked behind one of the narrow steel support columns that lined the platform, pressing herself against its cold metal surface as the footsteps drew closer. She frantically searched the platform for better cover, but there was nowhere else she could possibly hide.

If only she were more experienced in this kind

of thing. She still hadn't recovered enough since the park to gather up more than a stiff breeze. That meant she would have to rely on what weapons were closest at hand. Cally reached out with her mind and made contact with something brown, furry, and very nearby.

As the man reached the bottom of the stairs, a rat the size of a kitten darted out of nowhere, its beady eyes gleaming like tiny polished stones. The animal reared up on its hind legs and made an angry, squealing noise.

"What the hell—?!?" the stranger cried as the rat suddenly raced up his leg. *"Ah! Get off me! Help!"* He swatted at the angry rodent as it tore at him with its gleaming yellow teeth, but it refused to be frightened away and was at his throat within seconds. As he tried to shield his eyes from its slashing fangs and filthy claws, he lost his balance and toppled off the edge of the platform. On striking the ground below, the rat jumped off and scurried back into the darkness of the tunnel, leaving its victim lying dazed on the tracks, moaning as blood oozed from the numerous wounds to his face and hands.

Cally peered over the platform and, with a start, recognized the young man as the one she had seen earlier, the one with whom she had experienced an unexpected connection. The fear that she had for her own life suddenly turned into alarm. She had sicced the rat on the stranger, hoping she could run away while he was distracted. It hadn't occurred to her that he would end up seriously injured as a result of the attack.

"What have I done?" She groaned.

A distant rumbling, a burst of air, and a swirl of trash from the tunnel signaled an oncoming train. Realizing there was no time to lose, Cally leaped off the platform onto the wounded stranger below.

"Hold still! Don't move!" she shouted, pulling him more evenly between the rails.

"What are you doing?" he cried, his brown eyes wide with fear as Cally pressed her face as close to his as a lover's.

"Saving your life!" Cally could smell the blood leaking from his wounds and fought to ignore the hunger it aroused in her. This was no time to get distracted. "If you don't keep still, we're both gonna lose a leg in a second!"

The ground beneath them began to tremble as they lay there wrapped in each other's arms. The man-made thunder filled their ears and rattled their bones. Cally pressed her head against the young man's chest as he lay motionless beneath her, staring up at the speeding undercarriage of the subway cars passing inches above his face. After what seemed like an eternity, the train finally came to a stop above them.

"What do we do now?" he asked in a hoarse whisper.

"Wait until it leaves," Cally whispered back. "No one knows we're down here. Even if someone's on the platform, I doubt they could hear us if we yelled for help."

The young man didn't say anything but instead tightened his grip on Cally, pulling her as close to him as possible. As she listened to his heart pounding in his chest, she breathed in the scent of his skin. She found it strangely comforting, even soothing.

After a long minute the doors chimed closed and the subway train's wheels began to turn. Cally held perfectly still as the cars click-clacked by over her head, fearful that the slightest movement might end in disaster. She marveled at how warm the young man's flesh felt against her own. She closed her eyes and took another, deeper breath, savoring his smell so she could remember it later.

After the last car passed by, she finally lifted her head and looked around.

"It's okay," she said reassuringly. "You can let go of me now."

"And I was having such a wonderful time," he said with a weak laugh.

"We've got to get you out of here before another train shows up," Cally said as she stood up.

"Sounds like a good idea to me."

"Hello? Anybody there?" she called out. *"Man on the tracks!"*

Cally listened for a response, but all she heard was her own echo.

"Can you stand?" she asked.

"Yeah," he said, nodding. "I think so."

As Cally helped him to his feet, the young man grimaced and fell into her. She staggered slightly as his body became deadweight and then effortlessly scooped him into her arms. She easily jumped back onto the train platform, carrying him over one shoulder. Moving with the grace of a cat, she propped his body upright on a nearby bench and gently stroked his left cheek, wiping away a smear of blood.

"Hey! What are you doing there?"

A transit worker was hurrying toward them with an alarmed look. Suddenly realizing she was covered in grease and filth from the tracks, Cally figured he had mistaken her for a runaway trying to roll a commuter.

"My friend needs an ambulance," she said quickly. "I think he's hurt. He fell off the platform onto the tracks."

"Holy Christ! How'd he manage to get back up?"

"I went and got him."

The transit worker gave her a dubious glance. "A young lady like you dragged this guy back up onto the platform all by yourself? Gedoutta here!"

"I guess it must have been adrenaline or something," Cally said with a shrug. "You know, like that woman who picked up the car to save her kid."

"Oh, yeah! I remember reading about that." Apparently satisfied by Cally's explanation, the transit worker pulled a walkie-talkie out of his jacket pocket. "Central, this is Colina; I've got a situation here. Over." He hit the receive button, but all that came out of the earpiece was a howl of static. "The reception down here is crap. We're fifty feet under the street. I'll have to go to the upper concourse to make the call. Are you sure you'll be all right?"

"I'm perfectly fine. I'll keep an eye on him until you get back."

"Okay—wait right here!"

As the transit worker ran back up the stairs, the young man gave a low moan of pain. Cally placed a hand on his shoulder, gently restraining him as he attempted to sit upright.

"Take it easy. You must have busted something when you fell."

He took a deep breath and grimaced. "You're right," he groaned. "I think I might have cracked a rib or two." He lifted his head. "I owe you my life," he whispered, his brown eyes drinking in her lips, her face, her hair. "You didn't have to do what you did."

"My grandmother once told me the worst thing anyone can do is nothing."

"Your grandmother sounds like a very wise woman."

"She was," Cally agreed. "Besides, I'm sure you would have done the same for me if our roles were reversed."

Something flickered in the young man's eyes and he quickly looked away. "Perhaps you're right."

Cally turned toward the Brooklyn-bound side of the platform. "I think I hear my train coming."

"You're not going to leave me, are you?" he asked, reaching for her hand.

"Don't worry, there's an ambulance on the way. You'll be all right."

"Please—don't go. Stay with me."

"Look, I'm gonna get in a *lot* of trouble if I don't leave!" she said earnestly.

"But you haven't told me your name! I should at *least* know the name of the girl who saved my life, shouldn't I?"

"It's Cally."

"I like that." He smiled. "My name's Peter."

Cally returned his smile as she squeezed his hand. "I like that, too. Take care of yourself."

"I'll try."

Peter Van Helsing watched as Cally hopped inside the J train and waved good-bye from her window seat. As he raised a bloodied hand to return her farewell, he wondered how he would explain things to his father. Tonight had been his first solo mission; he had been assigned to watch the subway station nearest the park in case the target escaped Big Ike's crew.

He reached inside his denim jacket and withdrew the wooden stake hidden inside, tossing it in the trash can next to the bench, just as he had been trained to do. The EMTs would be there soon, and it wouldn't do to have outsiders sticking their noses into the family business.

CHAPTER 5

"Hurry up!" Oliver yelled over his shoulder as he ran from the park. "We've got to get back to the cars before the Van Helsings call in support!"

"But I broke my heel!" Carmen whined, limping after him like a hobbled horse.

Oliver bent down and snapped the heel off the remaining slingback. "There! Now they match again!"

"Those were my new Pradas!" she wailed.

"So you'll be well dressed when they drive a stake through your heart and cut off your head!" Oliver growled. "If you slow me down again, I *swear* I'll leave you behind for the Van Helsings to take care of! Don't think I won't!"

The look in Oliver's eyes made Carmen stop arguing. She kicked off the ruined shoes, her bare feet slapping against the pavement of the West Village streets as she hurried after him.

Sergei slowed his run down to a trot and looked around. "Where's Tanith?" he asked. "Did anyone see her?"

"The last time I saw her, she was with Jules," Melinda answered. "Ollie, have you seen Jules?"

"He went after Lilith—that's all I know," Oliver replied.

"It looks like we might have to fly out of here. Until Jules or Tanith shows up, there's no way we can get back into the cars," Melinda said, pointing across the street at the parked limousines they had arrived in. The Graves driver was leaning against the hood of the Mercedes, his arms crossed over his chest, staring into space, while the de Laval driver busied himself by polishing the windshield of his vehicle.

"*Fly?*" Carmen frowned. "Are you serious? I can only stay in winged form for five minutes, tops! It'll take at least twenty minutes to get back uptown!"

"I realize it's dangerous. None of us are particularly strong fliers yet," Melinda replied. "But we have to get home as fast as we can."

"But what if they've already deployed their interceptors?" Oliver asked anxiously. "I heard that Van Helsings have specially trained eagles and condors to take out vampires on the wing."

"I've heard that too," Carmen agreed. "My aunt says some of them even use pet gargoyles they've raised from eggs! *Gargoyles*, Melly! An eagle would be bad enough—how are we supposed to fight off a gargoyle in midair?"

"You're getting yourself worked up over nothing, Carm," Melinda said, trying to calm her down. "It's just rumors, that's all, urban myths, that kinda stuff."

"Yeah, well, I've heard that before. Lilith and Tanith said the same thing about Van Helsings, and *now* look what's happened." Carmen's voice was quivering. "All I know is that I'm scared, my feet hurt, and I want to go home!"

"Let me try talking to Tanith's chauffeur," Sergei suggested. "I've been dating her for a few months. Maybe he'll recognize my scent. . . ."

"Be careful," Oliver cautioned. "Undead might not have the same powers as the true-born, but they can still fuck you up."

Sergei walked across the street, heading for the Bentley. As he drew closer to the car, Tanith's chauffeur turned to face him.

"Dixon, it's me," Sergei said, raising his hand in greeting. "You know me, don't you? My friends and I just need to get inside the car, that's all. . . ."

With a deep growl like a guard dog warning off a prowler, the driver bared his fangs at Sergei. His eyes were flashing ruby red as he positioned himself between the intruder and the car.

"Whoa! No need to get upset!" Sergei immediately

stepped back. He looked over his shoulder at the others and shook his head. "It's no use. Dixon's not going to let anyone in that car unless they're of the Graves bloodline. The same goes for Jules's driver. We'll have to risk flying, gargoyles or no gargoyles."

"Maybe not!" Melinda said excitedly. "Here comes Jules!"

Sergei and the girls turned to see their friend limping toward them, an arrow sticking out of his upper-right thigh. Jules paused long enough to yank it free, snapping it in two like kindling, as his friends surged around him.

"Praise the Founders!" Carmen exclaimed, throwing her arms around his neck. "We were afraid you were dead!"

Jules gave her a squeeze.

"I knew those bastards couldn't catch you," Sergei said with a relieved chuckle.

"Where are Lilith and Tanith?" Melinda asked anxiously.

"You didn't see?" Jules replied, a surprised look on his face.

"Afraid not," Oliver admitted. "When you yelled, 'Van Helsings,' we got out of there as fast as we could."

"Jules—what happened?" Melinda whispered.

"Tanith's dead."

"Oh, no!" Carmen gasped, covering her mouth.

"What?" Sergei blinked in surprise. "Are you sure?"

"Yeah, I'm afraid so," Jules replied sadly. "She's gone, dude—I'm sorry."

"What about Lilith?" Carmen whimpered. "Is she okay?"

"I don't know," Jules said grimly. "I was hoping she was here with you."

"So what do we do now?" Melinda asked.

"I won't leave without Lilith," Jules said firmly. "We already lost Tanith; I won't lose her too."

Suddenly a large animal the size of an Irish wolfhound, its fur dripping wet, came loping up the middle of the street from the direction of the park. Blue eyes blazing, the tailless beast suddenly stood up on its hind legs and nuzzled Jules's face.

"Lili!" Jules threw his arms around her. "You made it!"

Suddenly standing there in Jules's arms—stark naked, her wet hair cascading down her back like a waterfall—Lilith hungrily searched for his lips.

"Oh, my!" Oliver's gaze said it all.

Jules quickly shed his jacket and handed it to Lilith.

"Sorry about that," she said sheepishly. "When will D&G make dresses shapeshifter proof?"

"I'm just glad you escaped unhurt," Jules said, pulling her close.

"We've got to get out of here quick," Lilith said. "I heard the Van Helsings talking. Their reinforcements will be here soon."

"It'll be a bit of a tight fit, but I think we can all squeeze into my limo," Jules said, motioning to his driver. "Marcel! We're leaving now!"

Marcel put away his polishing rag and nodded. *"Oui*, Monsieur Jules," he said as he opened the rear door for his master. Melinda, Oliver, Carmen, Jules, and Lilith packed into the backseat while Sergei rode with the driver.

"What about Tanith's driver?" Melinda asked. "Shouldn't we tell him to go home?"

Jules shook his head. "It can't be helped. He's undead. He won't obey anyone who doesn't have Graves blood in their veins."

As the car pulled away from the curb, Lilith wriggled her naked body around on Jules's lap so she could look out the rear window one last time at the chauffeur. Dixon leaned against the Bentley, arms folded, patiently awaiting his mistress's return. He would continue to do so until the rising sun turned him to ash.

The night doorman at the Balmoral didn't raise so much as an eyebrow as Lilith crossed the lobby barefoot, dressed in nothing but her boyfriend's jacket. After all, he was merely a servant. It wasn't his place to approve or disapprove of how a member of the family dressed.

Lilith entered the elevator and punched the button

for the penthouse floor, waiting until the doors shut securely behind her before allowing her hands to tremble.

During the whole ride back, she had worked hard to keep from appearing weak in front of the others. But the truth was, what happened in the park had shaken her badly. She had never seen anyone die before—and never suspected that the first death she would witness would be not just another vampire, but one of her best friends.

Tonight was a brutal reminder of how dangerous it was out there, especially for fledglings just learning to master the skills that would allow them to survive and prosper in a ruthless world.

Every time she closed her eyes, she saw Tanith lying sprawled on the ground like a broken toy. If she hadn't gotten out of the way at the very last second, she would have been the one lying there, not her friend. She frowned and shook her head, trying to dislodge what that meant from her mind.

It was all that damned New Blood's fault, she told herself. *If she hadn't attracted the Van Helsings' attention by summoning a storm, none of this would have happened.*

Lilith decided that the worst thing about the Van Helsings showing up and killing Tanith was that it broke up the fight between her and that New Blood trash. Sure, the girl caught her off guard with that whirl-wind, but Lilith was certain she would have won the fight in the end. It galled her that the newbie managed to escape unharmed. No doubt the little skank was telling all her lowlife friends about how she got one over on an Old Blood.

She could still hear the bitch's taunts ringing in her ears. Stormgatherer or not, there wasn't a newbie born fit to lick her shoes. Lilith promised herself that if she ever saw that hipster fashion victim again, she would tear her tongue out by the roots for even *daring* to speak to her!

Lilith stepped out of the elevator into the private lobby that served as the foyer for her apartment, only to find the family butler waiting for her.

"Greetings, Miss Lilith," he said in a cultured British accent, not reacting at all to her state of undress. "The master wishes to see you."

"Do I have to, Curtis?" Lilith groaned. "I've had a *really* shitty night, as you can no doubt see, and I'm really tired. . . ."

"Your father was most insistent that he see you as soon as you arrived. I have been standing here awaiting your return for"—the butler pulled a pocket watch from his waistcoat—"seven hours, twenty-six minutes, and fifty-eight seconds."

"Very well." Lilith sighed. Although the undead who served her family normally obeyed her every word, her father's wishes overrode hers every time.

"Come with me, Miss Lilith," Curtis said as he held open the front door. "The master is in his study."

Whatever her father's reason for wanting to speak to her, the fact that he was waiting for her in the study did not bode well. Although she'd lived in the penthouse all her life, Lilith could count on one hand the times she'd been inside his private sanctum.

Developer and CEO of HemoGlobe, the largest and most successful company in the blood bank industry, Victor Todd had single-handedly revolutionized vampire culture for true-born and undead alike.

Thanks to his processed blood supply program, paid for by monthly subscriptions, it was no longer necessary to spend every waking hour stalking and hunting that next meal. Now all but the most wretched had the time to focus on other needs and interests, using their free time to better their existence.

Yes, as far as the families of Lilith's friends and school-mates were concerned, Victor Todd was Thomas Edison, Henry Ford, and Bill Gates all rolled into one. But to Lilith, he was the man who controlled every aspect of her life, at least until she was finally old enough to marry Jules and begin her new life as the Countess de Laval.

As Curtis escorted her to her father, Lilith found herself glancing at the portraits that lined the long hallway. Her attention was momentarily caught by a painting of her grandparents, Adolphus Todesking and Marcilla Karnstein. Having died decades before she was born, they had never been anything more to her than daubs of paint on stretched canvas. The only thing Lilith really knew about them was that Adolphus was responsible for slaying Pieter Van Helsing after the legendary vampire hunter killed his beloved wife.

Lilith could almost swear Marcilla's head turned to watch her pass by.

Curtis hesitated before rapping lightly on the door to the study. "Miss Lilith has arrived home, sire."

"Send her in."

Lilith swallowed hard and tugged the lapels of her borrowed jacket even closer together. As much as she hated to admit it, deep down, at the very core of her being, she was afraid of Daddy.

Curtis held the door open but did not follow Lilith into the room. "Will there be anything else, Master Victor?" he asked.

"No. You're free to withdraw, Curtis."

"Thank you, master," the butler said, with more than a hint of relief in his voice as he closed the door, leaving Lilith alone with her father.

Victor Todd turned from the flat-panel computer monitor on his desk to face his daughter. With his money and brooding good looks, he was easily one of the most desirable men in the jet set.

"I trust you did not leave the house dressed like that, young lady?" He scowled.

"No, sir," Lilith replied, her voice suddenly very small. "If you're busy, I can come back later after I've changed clothes—"

"There's no need for that. I was simply checking on some investments I made in the foreign exchange market. The euro is doing very well right now," he said, self-satisfaction creeping into his voice despite his displeasure with his daughter. "Right now you and I need to talk. First I want to hear what you thought you were doing at the club last night; then you can explain how you ended up wearing *that*."

"You know about what happened at the Belfry?" Lilith asked, stalling for time.

"Of *course* I know!" he replied wearily. "I'm a co-owner of the club. You should know I have an interest in every vampire-friendly business in this city!"

"We were just having fun, that's all." Lilith dropped her eyes to the carpet. "It wasn't just me—Tanith and Carmen bit him too."

"I don't care what the others did or didn't do," Todd replied sternly. "They're not my daughters—you are."

"Yes, Father," Lilith said glumly.

"What possessed you to do something so reckless as to tap a human at the club in the first place? Never mind the security issues—did you even bother to consider whether you're ready to take responsibility for bringing unlife into this world?"

"That couldn't possibly have happened," Lilith said with a dismissive shrug. "I'm too young to create undead."

"Mercifully, that is still the case. But it won't be for much longer, Lilith. In the blink of an eye—another four years, five at the most—you'll finish maturing into an adult. You'll lose your ability to reflect, your aging process will slow to one tenth of a human's, and your bite will transform those you feed on into undead. . . ."

"Daddy, do we *have* to go through the 'bats and the bees' talk right now?" Lilith groaned, rolling her eyes in embarrassment.

"Better we discuss the matter now, before it's too late. I certainly can't trust your mother to handle the situation, can I?"

"No, sir," Lilith agreed.

Lilith couldn't remember the last time she had anything resembling a conversation with her mother. After spending over one hundred years trying desperately to conceive an heir for her husband, the former Irina Viesczy now spent as little time with her offspring and spouse as possible.

"Bringing undead into the world is serious business, Lili. They'll serve you without qualm or complaint for centuries. Odds are they'll even 'outlive' you and end up being passed down to your own heirs when the time comes, like Bruno and Esmeralda and Curtis. All of them will gladly kill and die for you. After all, if you're destroyed before you can pass along your bloodright—even to a usurper—they die as well. The undead are the true foundation on which power is based in our society.

"Remember, it is better to have crypts full of undead than vaults full of gold. Why? Because the vampire with the biggest bloodright gets the gold. It's that simple. But no matter how powerful I am, if you draw attention to us, you'll have to answer to the Synod. The man you attacked at the club is newsworthy, Lilith. What with satellite uplinks, podcasts, and CNN, it's more important than ever for our kind to keep our secret.

"If the Lord Chancellor finds you guilty of placing us in the spotlight, you'll be defanged."

"How barbaric!" Lilith gasped, instinctively covering her mouth.

"Indeed," her father replied. "In the old days it amounted to a death sentence, since the offender slowly starved to death. Now do you understand why it is wise to keep from doing things that would result in being brought before the Synod?"

"Yes, sir," she said sullenly.

"Not only that, but we also don't want to do anything that would make Count de Laval reconsider the wisdom of marrying into our family, am I right? So, do I have your promise that you will never tap a human in the club again?"

"Yes, sir."

"Very good," Todd said with a relieved sigh. "Now, perhaps you can tell me why you're standing in front of me dressed in nothing but a man's jacket. What happened to your dress?"

"It got shredded when I shapeshifted."

"You shapeshifted?" Todd scowled. "How did *that* happen?"

"It's a long story," Lilith replied, still staring at her feet.

"Why am I not surprised?"

"I'm sorry, Daddy. I really, really am. But it wasn't my fault," Lilith said, the words suddenly pouring out of her like water. "We were over at Tanith's place, just goofing off. We were bored because we couldn't go to the club. We ended up going to Washington Square Park. . . ."

"Whose bright idea was *that*?"

"Jules's."

At the mention of Jules, her father softened. "You were in the Village? What for?"

"We were just out partying, that's all, I promise."

"I know you're lying to me, Lilith. Or, at the very least, you're not telling me something. But I've had a *very* long night and I'm too tired to play any more games with you." He leaned toward his intercom. "If you don't tell me what you and the others were doing in the Village, I'm going to have all your credit cards canceled."

"No! Don't do that!"

"Then tell me the truth."

"Okay. You win," she said, her shoulders dropping in defeat. "We were slumming."

Victor Todd came out of his chair as if it were electrified. "You were *what*?" His voice reverberated so loudly it made the walls of the room shake. "Of all the most dangerous, *stupidest* things you could have done—! And after *everything* I have worked to achieve—! The whole *point* of HemoGlobe is to make risky behavior like that a thing of the past for our people! By the Founders, child, *what* were you thinking?"

"We thought it was safe this time. . . ."

"Safe! It's like Russian roulette—the odds are against you! Every time you go out in public, you run the risk of being attacked by Van Helsings! You, of all people, know how much you stand out in a crowd!"

"We were keeping a low profile, I swear! Everything was going just fine. Then this New Blood bitch showed up and everything got out of hand. . . ."

"New Blood?" Todd's scowl deepened further.

"Yeah. She's the one who's really responsible for what happened. If it wasn't for her, the Van Helsings would never have known we were there."

"What did she do?"

"She tried to attack me with a bolt of lightning."

"A *stormgatherer*?" Todd seemed genuinely startled by this revelation. "Are you *sure* about that? I thought you said the girl was a New Blood."

"Well, I *assumed* that's what she was," Lilith said. "I mean, I know all the Old Blood kids, and I've *never* seen this girl before. . . ."

"Then what happened?"

"Tanith got staked," Lilith replied, her voice dropping to little more than a whisper.

"By the Founders," Todd muttered in shock. "Is she—?"

Lilith nodded.

"I see," Todd said. He rubbed his lower lip with the knuckle of his right index finger, a sign that he was lost in his own thoughts. "Very well. Go on to bed, Lilith. I'll see that Dorian and Georgina are notified."

Victor Todd watched his daughter head out the door of the study. As she moved to shut the door behind her, Lilith looked over her shoulder at him, her brilliant blue eyes shining with tears.

"Daddy?" she asked in a wavering voice.

"Yes, Lilith?" he replied gently.

"You're not going to cut up my credit cards, are you?"

"No, princess." He sighed. "Of course not."

CHAPTER 6

C ally lived with her mother on the top floor of a
seven-story building that had originally been a
warehouse for pipe organs or something equally
Victorian. Their condo was one of many created for
the artists, students, and office workers forced out of
the Lower East Side in search of affordable rents.

Compared to some of the places they'd lived, the
three-bedroom-two-bath apartment they now called
home was a palace. Indeed, the living room had
excellent views and a large balcony that looked out
toward the Williamsburg Bridge. The kitchen was
outfitted with all stainless steel Viking appliances,
including a six-burner stove—not that it mattered,
since Cally's mom had no idea how to cook and no
intention of ever learning.

As she exited the elevator onto her floor, Cally

could hear the rumble from the home theater system's subwoofer. She sighed and rolled her eyes. No doubt they were going to get another nasty note from the condo board.

Cally's mother, Sheila Monture, was seated on the antique red velvet fainting couch facing the sixty-inch plasma flat-panel HDTV, watching, yet again, Francis Ford Coppola's *Dracula*. Cally recognized the scene as the one where Anthony Hopkins and Keanu Reeves charge into Winona Ryder's bedroom and catch her in the arms of Gary Oldman.

"I'm home!" Cally shouted over the thunderously loud sound track as she unlocked the door. She noticed that the draperies covering the huge picture windows in the living room had been pulled back so her mother could look out at the East River.

Sheila Monture spun around, startled by her daughter's sudden appearance. She fumbled with the remote, and the sound level on the movie dropped from deafening to merely loud.

"Sweetheart! There you are—! I was hoping you'd get home early enough for us to talk!"

As her mother rose to greet her, Cally saw that she was wearing a pale lavender negligee with stylized bat wing sleeves and a long black wig with a white streak in it. Over the years, Cally had come to recognize that her mother chose costumes to express her moods. Whenever she wanted to come across as sophisticated and aloof, she dressed like Morticia Addams; when she wanted to be perceived as motherly and down-to-earth, she dressed as Lily Munster.

"Talk? About what?" Cally asked warily.

"I heard from your father tonight," Sheila said cheerily, ignoring her daughter's tone of voice.

"A lot *he* cares!" Cally sneered.

"Now, darling, that's *not* true!" Sheila Monture affected an exaggerated frown as she clasped her hands over her breast. "Your father cares quite a bit about you."

Cally walked across the living room and stared out the window at the bridge, its metal span illuminated against the night.

"Darling, your father is giving you a big chance. Starting Monday, you are going to Bathory Academy," her mother said, clearly savoring the words.

Cally spun around in disbelief. "Why do I have to go there, of all places? I made the *honor roll* at Varney Hall last year!"

"That's the thing, sweetie. Your father's a *very* important, *very* busy man. He doesn't always have the time to deal with things himself. Normally, I send your report cards to the people who handle his business affairs for him, so it took your father a while before he got a chance to really look at your academic records. But once he did, he was *very* impressed. He told me tonight that you were being wasted at Varney. It's nice enough and all, but it's still a *New Blood* school. Your father wants to help you better yourself! Isn't that *wonderful*?"

Cally shook her head in furious denial. "You can tell him to forget it! I have friends at Varney. I am *not* going to that Old Blood bimbo house!"

Sheila Monture's too-wide smile faltered and she began to wring her hands, which was never a good sign. "But you *have* to, Cally. If you don't, your father will withdraw his protection, not to mention his money. We'll have to move again."

Cally put her hands to her head as if trying to keep it from exploding. "Move? I thought you said you bought this condo with the money Granny left you."

"I used those funds to make the down payment, but it's your father who pays the monthly note on the mortgage and all the other fees."

"Perhaps this would *mean* something to me if I knew who the hell my father actually *is*!" Cally snapped. "I've never seen the man or heard his voice! I don't even know his *name*! All I know is that he's too busy and important to spend time with me, he's married to someone else, and he's ashamed to acknowledge me!"

"Cally, *please* don't talk that way," her mother pleaded. "It's not fair to blame him for how things are between you. My mother had a lot to do with keeping your father away from you, and you know that. Believe me, when your father is ready to reveal himself to you, he will do so. Until then, it's safer that you not know his identity. Your father is a *powerful* man, with *powerful* enemies, ones who would stop at *nothing* to make sure they destroy his posterity."

"Is that all I am to him, then? A hedge against extinction?"

Sheila Monture was about to deny her daughter's assessment, then thought better of it and quickly looked away. Cally groaned in disgust.

"Yeah, that's what I thought. If you need me for anything, I'll be in my room."

As Cally moved toward the hallway, Sheila grabbed her daughter by the wrist. "Please, Cally—I beg you, *please* do as your father asks. I don't want to move! I *like* it here in Williamsburg, and I know you do too! The artist community here is very open-minded. I'm *comfortable* here. It's a lot like the East Village used to be. Nobody stares at me when I go out, at least not too much. I don't want to *have* to move again and end up someplace where the neighbors treat us like freaks."

"Mom, *don't* put this on me—it's not fair."

"*Please*, Cally?" Sheila asked in a quavering voice. The tears welling at the corners of her eyes were already making her mascara run. "Just go along and do this *one* little thing for Mama . . . ?"

Cally clenched her jaw and told herself she was not going to give in. Not this time. She tried to pull her wrist free, but her mother wouldn't let go. It would be very easy to *make* her let go, but Cally had no desire to truly hurt her. Her mother was damaged enough already.

She took a deep breath and let it out in a long, pained sigh. "Okay, Mom. You win. I'll go."

CHAPTER 7

T he Van Helsing Institute was headquartered in a
rambling Georgian estate set on seventeen acres
in the horse country of Connecticut. For the last
eighteen and a half years it had been Peter Van Helsing's
home and school. In time, he would no doubt take over
the reins of the company, following in the footsteps of
his ancestors. Or so he thought until he crossed Cally's
path.

Peter moved gingerly across the room to the huge
mahogany desk in front of the fireplace. If he walked
too fast, his newly cracked rib made it feel like someone
was jabbing him in the side with a spear. He was glad
his father wasn't around, because he still wasn't sure
what he was going to tell him about what happened.

Peter glanced up at the portrait of his great-great-
great-grandfather hanging over the mantelpiece. Dressed

in a dark cravat worn with a wide turnover collar that was fashionable in the 1830s, the infamous Pieter Van Helsing seemed to regard his most recent descendant with a disapproving stare.

A twinge of guilt almost as sharp as the pain in his ribs caused Peter to look away. He dropped his eyes to the sea of folders filled with printouts, reports, photographs, and newspaper clippings that covered the desktop. Even though much of what was in the aging manila binders had long since been digitized and transferred into the Institute's computer system, his father was an old-fashioned man and preferred having the actual documentation close at hand.

As Peter moved closer, he heard the sound of chains rattling. The gargoyle lifted its head from the rug by the fireplace with a growl so deep Peter felt it more than heard it. About the size and general build of a bull mastiff, the creature had leathery, grayish-green skin and batlike wings growing from its shoulders. It sniffed the air, and the rumbling growl disappeared, replaced by a friendly whine of recognition.

"Do you want a treat, Talus?"

The gargoyle's hairless, lizardlike tail began to slap against the rug in anticipation as Peter flipped open the lid of an old wooden cigar box. He plucked one of the dead mice from inside by its tail and tossed it to the drooling beast. Talus snapped the morsel out of midair, then looked back expectantly at Peter.

"One's enough." Peter laughed, wagging a finger in admonishment. "I don't want Dad blaming me for ruining your supper!"

As if on cue, the doors to the office opened and Christopher Van Helsing, president and CEO of the Van Helsing Institute, the world's oldest secular supernatural extermination service, entered the room. With his shock of wavy gray hair and the intense, deeply preoccupied look he always seemed to wear, he bore an uncanny resemblance to Beethoven.

"Peter!" Van Helsing said, hurrying forward to greet his wounded son. "My brave boy! How are your ribs?"

"Not too bad, I guess," Peter said, wincing at his father's embrace. "The doctors at the emergency room said I cracked one pretty good, but nothing's actually broken. I'm going to the infirmary in a bit to have Doc Willoughby tape me up. I'm just waiting for him to finish taking care of Big Ike and Drummer."

"I'm glad to hear you're okay. In any case, it's a good thing we Van Helsings heal pretty fast, eh, son?" his father said.

"Yes, sir," Peter agreed.

"Are you up to talking about what happened in the subway?"

"I guess so, sir." Peter shrugged.

"Is something the matter?" Van Helsing frowned, surprised by Peter's lack of enthusiasm. "The last time

I saw you, you were all pumped up about going solo for the first time."

"It's just that you were counting on me, and I feel like I let you down, sir."

"It's not just *your* fault the mission failed, son," his father replied. "The whole thing was a cock-up."

"Yes, sir," Peter murmured, his eyes dropping to the floor.

"Speaking of which . . ." Van Helsing strode over to his desk and punched the intercom. "Tell Rémy I want to see him in my office. Stat."

"Yes, sir," a female voice replied. "He's on his way."

As Peter's father moved to sit down, Talus perked up.

"Who's happy to see Daddy?" Van Helsing asked as he scratched behind the beast's batlike ears. "Yes, it's *you*, Talus! *You're* happy to see Daddy, aren't you?"

"I just gave him a treat," Peter warned his father. "Don't let him trick you into thinking he's starving."

"I'm a sucker when it comes to this beast, and he knows it," Van Helsing said with an uncharacteristic chuckle. "It's hard not to get attached when you hatch them yourself."

There was a light knock as Rémy stuck his head inside the office door. "You wanted to see me, boss?"

Van Helsing nodded and motioned for the other man to enter. His smile was gone, replaced by a scowl. "Indeed I do, Rémy. I sent you and the others out on what should have been a relatively simple ambush—of a young girl, no less. I would like you to tell me how it is my best field operative is in critical condition after being electrocuted, my strike team leader has a dislocated shoulder, and my son is covered in rat bites and suffering from a busted rib."

Rémy swallowed so hard his Adam's apple nearly disappeared. "Boss, I can explain what happened! We had things under control, but before we could move to take down the target, a group of oldies showed up. . . ."

Van Helsing raised an eyebrow. "Adults or fledglings?"

"Fledglings, as far as any of us could tell. They seemed about the same age as the stormgatherer. There were at least three suckers. A male and two females."

"Slummers, no doubt." Van Helsing shook his head in disgust.

"One of the females mixed it up with the target. That's what triggered everything. Next thing we know, we're in the middle of a whirlwind. Big Ike made the call to take out the Old Bloods before they could gang up on the stormgatherer."

"Did he succeed?"

Rémy nodded. "He managed to stake one of the females. The trophy's being cleaned and prepared as we speak. After that, things went haywire. The stormgatherer ended up attacking Ike. Then the male stepped in—or flew in, rather. We wounded him, but not before he tried to yank Drummer's arm off."

"What about the second female?"

"She managed to escape. Like I said, boss, we had everything under control until the Old Bloods showed up."

"I see," Van Helsing said. "What about you, Peter? Was the sucker who attacked you in the subway the same one Drummer reported seeing in the park? Was she the stormgatherer?"

"I'm not sure," Peter said, shifting uneasily. "It all happened so fast. I barely had a chance to look at her before the rat jumped me."

"Did you see which train she was taking? Was she on the uptown or downtown platform?"

"Uptown," Peter said quickly. "She was definitely headed uptown."

"Very interesting," Van Helsing said, jotting down a note.

"Are you *sure* this girl is the one you've been looking for?" Peter asked as he watched his father take in the misinformation. Why had he lied? Peter didn't like the feeling, yet he felt compelled to do it for Cally.

"Son, I've never been surer of anything in my life. Rémy, do you have any undercover agents working outside of Manhattan?"

"I've got operatives keeping tabs on this club in Williamsburg the stormgatherer was spotted at a few weeks back."

"Good. Have them reassigned to Midtown and the Upper East Side. If the grandmother is no longer in the picture, odds are the girl's become close with the father. Since we know who he is, it'll be easier to keep him under surveillance. He'll eventually lead us to her."

"Yes, boss." Rémy turned and hurried out of the office.

Peter glanced over at his father, who was scowling at the fragments of information scattered across his desk. Christopher Van Helsing pushed the various pieces of paper around with his forefinger, as if trying to put together a jigsaw puzzle. Peter knew all too well that his father could go for hours without speaking when he was in one of his moods.

"I better be going too, Dad."

"No. Stay and talk to me, boy," his father replied without looking up. "We're close. Very close. Your grandfather, rest his soul, taught me that the most valuable tool in a vampire hunter's arsenal is his intuition. And mine tells me that we're on the right track, son. I can feel it in my bones. The stormgatherer is the one we've been looking for.

"She's the right age. And I can assure you, from personal experience, that the old woman could throw bolts with the best of them. It only makes sense that her ability would be passed along to her granddaughter, if not amplified.

"If this girl is who I think she is—if she is *what* I think she is—then she is the greatest weapon the Van Helsing Institute has had the opportunity to use against the vampire race since Pieter himself."

"But what if she isn't willing to help us? What happens then?"

"If she or her grandmother, assuming the old woman's still alive, proves hostile to our plans, they will have to be terminated."

Peter blinked in surprise. "But I thought the grandmother was an old friend of yours."

"That's true," Van Helsing said, a flicker of regret crossing his face. "I've known Sina Monture since I was a boy. She joined the Elites back when your grandfather Leland was running things. She was one of the most powerful white witches ever to work for the Institute.

"Sina was married to Cyril Monture, your grandfather's best friend and my godfather. Neither one of them was what you'd call young, so we were all surprised when Sheila was born.

"They spoiled the baby rotten, and of course she

grew up to be one of those kids attracted to every-thing their parents are against. She was fascinated with vampires. Spent all her time watching movies about them, reading books about them—eventually, she went out looking for them. She even managed to find her-self a vampire lover.

"Poor Cyril had a massive heart attack when he saw his daughter being carried away by that fiend. He died in my arms.

"Sina was never the same after that. Then, two years later, without any warning, she quit the Insti-tute. We had all assumed Sheila had been turned into one of the undead, but it seems the sucker kept her as his mistress. When she became pregnant with his half-breed baby, she decided to reconcile with her mother.

"I realized the child's potential as a weapon immedi-ately and contacted Sina. She threatened to use her powers against me if I ever came near her or her grand-child. I knew then that the woman I once knew had been irreversibly corrupted, as are all who traffic with vampires and their spawn."

"But—termination? Is there no other way?" Peter asked, trying not to show his revulsion.

"Better that than to have the girl fall into the hands of our enemies."

* * *

Peter's head was swimming as he left his father's office. As a young boy he had told the usual fibs kids tell their parents. But what he had just done was far more serious than lying about stealing cookies or playing ball in the house.

Up until this point in his life, all Peter had ever really wanted was to hunt down and destroy vampires, just like his father and his grandfather before him, going back five generations. Less than twenty-four hours ago he had been so excited about carrying out his first solo mission he'd barely been able to sleep. But now all he could think about was Cally.

He could still feel the weight and warmth of her body pressed against his own. Whenever he closed his eyes, he saw her face looking out at him from the window of the Brooklyn-bound train, smiling as she waved good-bye.

Peter was both thrilled and frightened by the strength of the emotions coursing through him. His father claimed that vampires were capable of corrupting even the purest heart, given enough exposure. But that couldn't possibly apply to her, could it? She wasn't like the others. The fact that he was alive proved it.

He needed to see her again the way a tiger needs to quench its thirst. But how? He knew she was living in Brooklyn, but where exactly? Suddenly he remembered Rémy mentioning a club in Williamsburg she'd been spotted at that was under surveillance. It shouldn't be difficult to find out the name of the place—he just had to ask Rémy for the information. After all, who would suspect the boss's son, of all people, of being in love with a vampire?

CHAPTER 8

Because the Graveses were out of the country and Lilith had been their daughter's closest friend, tradition dictated that she be the one to host Tanith's totentanz, where everyone gathered to exchange token sympathies and then sing, dance, and drink in memory of their fallen comrade, all the while laughing in the face of death.

Back in the day, the parties would go for weeks. But given the short notice and the fact that everyone was just so *busy* nowadays, Tanith's totentanz was, by necessity, limited to a single night.

"There you are!" Sebastian said, his face pulled into an approximation of sympathy. "I was absolutely *horrified* when I heard what happened, sweetie!"

"Thank you, Seb," Lilith replied as they exchanged

air kisses. "It was sweet of you to agree to hold Tanith's totentanz here."

"It's the least I can do, darling, considering the circumstances." Sebastian sighed. "Besides, Sunday is a slow night."

Thanks to email and IM, news of Tanith's end at the hands of the Van Helsings had spread like wildfire through the popular kids of both Bathory Academy and Ruthven's as well as among many of the older, recently matured graduates. Lilith looked around the club at all the beautiful young men and women drinking snifters of laced blood.

"It's great to have such a strong turnout on such short notice," she said.

"Ooh! Rene, look! There's Lilith!"

Lilith turned her head in the direction of the squeal and sighed as she saw Rene Grimshaw and Bianca Mortimer bearing down on her.

Pasting an all-purpose smile on her face, she said, "Glad you could make it."

"Oh, we wouldn't have missed this for the world, Lili!" Rene exclaimed. "I mean, *everyone* who is *anyone* is here!"

"I'm sure Tanith would appreciate it," Lilith said dryly.

"Ooh! Lilith! Is it true you were there when Tanith was killed?" Bianca asked, her eyes gleaming with ghoulish fascination.

Rene leaned forward expectantly, like a robin waiting for a worm. "Ooh! Was it gross? Do you think it hurt?"

"I don't know," Lilith replied, taken aback by the barrage of questions. "It all happened so fast. . . ."

"Weren't you scared?"

Before Lilith had a chance to answer, Bianca nudged Rene, pointing across the room. "Isn't that Dustin Grabstein? The one you have the crush on?"

"Oh. My. Gods." Rene giggled, all but swooning.

"Come on!" Bianca said, tugging on her friend's arm. "Let's go talk to him!"

"Bye, Lilith!" Rene called over her shoulder. "See you at school tomorrow night!"

Sebastian laughed as he watched Bianca and Rene totter off. "Don't let those bubble heads bother you. I'm making sure all Tanith's *truly* close friends are escorted upstairs, love."

When she got to the Loft, Jules rose to meet her, his eyes luminescent in the dim light.

"Sorry I'm late," she said.

"I would have ordered you a drink, but I didn't want it to coagulate before you got here. I'll go get it for you. . . ."

Lilith was surprised by how considerate Jules was acting; it felt good. Sitting down on the sofa next to Melinda to wait for Jules, it took her a moment or two to realize who was missing.

"Has anyone seen Sergei?" Lilith asked.

"He's around here somewhere," Oliver said vaguely.

Lilith wondered if Sergei was upset. Suddenly images of Tanith's body lying crumpled on the ground began to flash through her mind's eye. Then Tanith's face became her own.

Horrified, Lilith glanced down at her hands and saw that they were trembling. "Please excuse me for a moment," she said, snatching up her purse.

As Lilith hurried to the ladies' room, she felt a sort of panic starting to set in.

Even though she knew it made no sense, she needed to see her own face looking back out at her to reassure herself that she wasn't the one who was dead. She just needed a little peek, that's all.

As she opened the door to the ladies' room, she automatically scanned the floor beneath the toilet stalls to see if any of them were occupied. A pair of masculine legs was clearly visible in the farthest stall, black leather pants pooled atop his boots.

At first Lilith thought one of the male partygoers was too wasted to realize he was in the ladies' room. Then she heard heavy breathing coming from the stall, followed by the sound of a woman's voice moaning in ecstasy. Lilith smiled and nodded, her anxiety momentarily forgotten. What better way to spit in the face of death than to screw during a totentanz?

Listening to the mystery lovers was starting to arouse her. After she was finished looking in the mirror, she would go find Jules and see if he was as adventurous as the owner of the black leather pants.

The stall began to violently vibrate, as if the couple on the other side was trying to knock the door off its hinges. The female's cries suddenly became feverish, while the male groaned. A moment later, a second pair of legs, these decidedly feminine, dropped into sight, and the stall door swung open.

Lilith wondered if she should duck into the other stall, for modesty's sake, but decided not to bother. Her curiosity was piqued and she was dying to discover the identities of the mystery lovers. Besides, how much privacy could you possibly expect while fucking in a public restroom?

A tall, thin girl with long, black hair tottered out of the stall on a pair of wedges as she yanked the bodice of her dress back up over her exposed breasts. Lilith instantly recognized her as Samara Bleak, one of her classmates at Bathory. Samara froze the moment she saw Lilith, a look of stunned surprise on her face. A second later Samara's partner exited the stall, still pulling up his leather trousers.

"Sergei—! What the hell?" Lilith exclaimed.

"Oh, hi, Lilith," Sergei said with a hazy, post-coital smile. "You know Samara, right?"

"I best be going," Samara said, scurrying out the door.

"Sergei—what are you doing?" Lilith stared in disbelief as he zipped up his fly. "Tanith hasn't been dead forty-eight hours and you're already fooling around with someone else?"

"I was fond of Tanith." Sergei shrugged. "But it was never serious. She would not expect me to stay brokenhearted."

"You'd have to *be* brokenhearted first in order to *stay* brokenhearted!" Lilith snapped.

"What I had with Tanith was fun," Sergei said. "But now it is over, never to return. There will be others who will make me feel the same way she did. You need to get with the spirit of the totentanz, Lili."

"You're such a pig, Sergei!" Lilith spat as she exited the ladies' room, slamming the door behind her.

She strode angrily across the salon, motioning for the bartender to set her up with another drink.

She took a deep draught of the laced blood, only to grimace in distaste. She pushed the drink aside and turned back to rejoin the others, nearly colliding with Jules. His smile quickly disappeared as he saw the look on her face.

"Is something wrong?"

"You mean *besides* Tanith being dead and never, *ever* coming back again?" she replied, loudly enough that those closest to them fell silent and stared at her. "Oh, I'm *sorry*," Lilith said to the sea of vaguely familiar faces gawking at her. "I didn't mean to interrupt the party."

"They're just doing what she would have done," Jules said. "Tanith loved partying more than anyone. You know that. She would have wanted it this way. None of us can change what happened. All we can do is just keep on like we did before and not let it change us."

"I know." Lilith sighed. "I guess I'm still upset, that's all."

"Jules! My man! How's it hanging?"

"Huh? Oh, hey, Sergei," Jules replied, momentarily distracted by his friend's arrival.

"Forget it, then," Lilith snarled, flashing Sergei a look as black and sharp as volcanic glass. "I'm going home."

"What's up with her?" Sergei asked. "Was it something I said?"

Sunday was laundry night in the Monture household. While stripping the bedclothes from her mother's bed earlier that evening, Cally had found yet another shut-off notice from Con Ed stuffed under the mattress, where Sheila habitually hid things she didn't want to deal with. The laundry would have to wait.

Cally didn't have the money she'd planned on from the park and needed to make up the difference if she wanted to keep the lights on. Since the Van Helsings had made the park too hot for comfort, she would have to stick closer to home. And there was only one place in Billyburg where she could find the type of prey she needed: Underbelly.

Cally went to her room and rummaged through her closet in search of something sexy to wear. She finally settled on a yellow satin miniskirt with a green corset bodice that she knew showed off her alabaster shoulders and shapely legs to their best advantage. She then slipped on the new pair of Miu Miu heels she'd snapped up last week at the consignment store off Bedford Avenue.

Once she was dressed, she put on eyeliner and lipstick like her grandmother had taught her, using only her delicate fingers as a guide. Once she was finished, she sneaked a quick peek in the compact she kept in her vintage clutch purse, just to make sure everything was on straight.

As she walked through the living room, she saw that her mother was engrossed in yet another movie. This time she was watching *The Brides of Dracula*.

"I need to go out. I'll be back in a few hours, Mom," Cally said, trying to make herself heard over the 5.1 Dolby.

"Be careful, sweetheart," Sheila Monture replied, waving good-bye without bothering to look away from the flat screen.

Located in the basement of a converted mayonnaise factory, Underbelly was the kind of club where identification was rarely checked, the drinks were poured strong, and drugs freely passed hands—in short, it was a good place to prey.

The doorman barely gave her a second look as she entered the club. She ordered a drink at the bar, then pretended to sip it as she scanned the room.

Even on a Sunday, it was crammed with international scenesters, young models, and Williamsburg hipsters with paint-speckled pants and arms swarming with tattoos.

"Cally! Where have you been keeping yourself?"

She turned to smile at Simon Magi, an old school friend from Varney Hall. He squeezed her arm in his friendly way, pointing to Cindy Darko, who was calling them over to one of the dimly lit booths that lined the walls of the bar.

"We haven't heard from you all weekend," Cindy said. "How come you're not answering messages?"

"Oh, I've been around," Cally said, sliding into the booth opposite them. "I ran into trouble across the river the other night. Washington Square Park is crawling with Van Helsings."

"Are you okay?" Simon asked, his face showing concern.

"Yeah. I got away clean. But I did see someone else get staked while I was there."

"Founders have mercy!" Cindy gasped, covering her mouth in surprise. "Was it anyone we know?"

"No," Cally replied, shaking her head. "It was some oldie."

Simon and Cindy exchanged a relieved look. "Praise the Founders for that, at least." Cindy sighed.

"So, are you ready for that big test in Mr. Dirge's luring class this week?" Simon asked.

"Yeahhh. About that." Knowing how intense the rivalry was between dear old Varney Hall and Bathory Academy, Cally knew she was heading into rough waters. "I've been going through changes the last couple of nights. . . ."

"How so?"

"It seems my asshole dad has made big plans for me."

"Your dad?" Simon frowned. "The one you've never met?"

"That's the one." Cally took a deep breath. She knew there was no putting it off. She might as well tell them and get it over with. "He's decided to 'better my education' by sending me to Bathory Academy."

"You've gotta be shitting me!" Simon's face suddenly drew itself tight.

"I wish I was. Tomorrow's my first night. I've got to wear a school uniform and everything. This afternoon he had the uniforms delivered to the apartment. I hope you never see me in it." Cally grimaced in distaste.

"But Bathory's an Old Blood school!" Cindy exclaimed, stating the obvious.

"It was tough enough at Varney Hall—I can only imagine how welcome I'm going to be at Bathory. But I've got to do it."

"Yeah, well, good luck with that," Simon said, already a former friend. "Speaking of school, Cindy and I better get going."

"Huh?" Cindy said, surprised by Simon's sudden announcement. "Going where? It's still early. . . ."

"You remember, Cindy," Simon said, dragging her out of the booth by her elbow. "We've got that exam in undead management tomorrow."

"We do? Oh! Right! We do!"

"That's okay. I understand," Cally said as they hurried off.

She'd dared to hope for more support from Simon and Cindy and was hurt and disappointed by their response. But even Cally felt like a traitor to the New Bloods, who had once been her closest friends.

"Do you mind if I have a seat?"

Cally looked up from her dark thoughts and was surprised to see a familiar face smiling down at her.

"What are *you* doing here?" she gasped as Peter slid into the booth.

"Waiting for you to show up."

"Are you *stalking* me?" Cally asked, not sure whether to be pleased or alarmed. "How did you know I'd be here?"

"I have my ways of getting information," he replied, flashing her a look that suggested it wasn't a joke.

Cally cocked her head in disbelief. "You've been lounging around expecting me to show up? Why would you do *that*?"

"So I could thank you for saving my life."

"You did that the other night."

"Would you rather I leave?" he asked.

Cally looked into Peter's eyes and felt a pull of attraction even stronger than the first time their gazes locked. "No," she admitted. It was kind of ironic that he'd shown up just as Simon and Cindy had gone away. "To tell you the truth," she said with a crooked smile, "I'm actually kind of glad to see you."

"I was hoping you'd say that." Peter smiled, taking her hands in his own. "Cally—I have a confession to make. Ever since I met you, I can't get you out of my head. I don't understand what I'm feeling. But do you feel it too?"

"You don't know who I am," Cally whispered, not wanting it to end.

Peter's smile faltered and he quickly looked away, unable to meet her eyes.

"I know more than you think I do. . . . I never told you my full name, Cally. I was afraid to."

"Afraid?" Cally's heart began to beat like a hummingbird caught in a spider's web. "Why would you be afraid of me?"

"Because I thought you would kill me if you knew who I really was."

As she listened to Peter's words, Cally knew she didn't want to hear what he had to say. She glanced about uneasily as she tried to regain her composure and force her lips back into a smile. "Why would I want to kill you? That's crazy talk."

"Cally, my name is Peter Van Helsing."

Cally sat there for a long moment.

"I have to leave," she said numbly, pulling her hands free.

As she began to get up, he grabbed at her, snaring her by the wrist. "Cally, it's not what you think! You're in no danger! I'm not going to hurt you!"

"Leave me alone!" she snapped, jerking free of his grasp. "Stay away from me, Peter! I don't want to hurt you, but I will if I have to!"

Then she was gone.

* * *

Cally ran down Metropolitan Avenue, angrily knuckling the tears from her eyes. On some unconscious level she must have known he was a Van Helsing right from the start. What really aggravated her was how clichéd the whole damn thing was: vampire and vampire hunter falling for each other at first sight. How much lamer could it possibly be? She was just as pathetic as her mother. But at least her mom knew what she was getting into right from the start—even sought it out, in fact.

As far as Cally was concerned, there was nothing sicker and more disgusting than loving someone dedicated to the systematic genocide of your people, except, by all that was unholy, hoping that she might see him again.

Cally's mother was waiting for her just inside the door when she came home.

"There you are, sweetheart! Tomorrow's going to be a very important night for you, so I want you to make sure you get a good day's sleep! That means no staying up late to watch *The View*, young lady!" Sheila threw her arms around her daughter, hugging her tight. "You *won't* regret it, I promise! You'll see—it will all be for the better!"

"Yeah. Whatever." Cally sighed as she peeled herself free of her mother's embrace. "I'm going to take a shower before I go to bed."

Cally's room was at the end of the hallway. She slammed the door shut behind her and kicked off her shoes. As if the events of the night weren't already upsetting enough, the first thing she saw was one of the Bathory Academy uniforms draped across the foot of her bed, like the empty skin of a serpent.

CHAPTER 9

T here is nothing about Bathory Academy's exterior
to suggest that its students are fledgling vampires.
There's no outward sign of the strange nature of
its teachings—unless you count its eternally shuttered
windows. Beautifully designed, the three-story mansion
on East Ninety-first Street was built by one of the old
robber barons, back when the Upper East Side was still
the suburbs. In fact, the only building in the vicinity
that dates back as far as Bathory Academy is its male
counterpart, Ruthven's School for Boys, located two
streets over on East Eighty-ninth.

Every Monday through Thursday night, from late
September until early May, a succession of limousines
pull up in front of the school, disgorging a steady
stream of young girls dressed in maroon blazers and
gray pleated skirts. What they do inside the school

is anybody's guess. Most nights the students remain inside the building until at least two in the morning, sometimes as late as four. Every so often groups of students leave in the company of what are assumed to be faculty members, whisked away in shiny stretch limos on mysterious midnight field trips.

These sightings aside, the girls and their teachers have remained little more than phantoms to the generations of New Yorkers who have found themselves neighbors to the school. And since those who do not mind their own business have a tendency to suddenly disappear forever, it's far safer for all concerned to simply explain away Bathory Academy as a private night school for the children of the pampered rich who cannot be bothered to get up at the crack of dawn and prefer to sleep away the daylight hours in their parents' penthouses.

Getting dressed was one of Cally's favorite things. She'd always had a flair for styling clothes. Ever since she was old enough to talk, she had been allowed to dress however she pleased, or at least as far as her pocketbook permitted. She loved buying unusual fabrics, ribbons, and lace and using them to customize the skirts and dresses she found at vintage shops and flea markets.

As she checked herself in the mirror, she regarded the dreadful maroon blazer and gray skirt with disgust. It was so drab and nondescript compared to what she usually wore. More than ever she wished she was human and could have a tattoo! Sadly, vampires healed so fast the ink was literally pushed out of the skin within seconds of being applied. Perhaps there was another, less drastic way of proclaiming her individuality on her first night at her new school?

She opened the jewelry box on her vanity table and took out a pair of vintage Bakelite bangles she inherited from her grandmother. One was a pale olive color that could almost pass for jade; the other was sunflower yellow.

"That's better," she said with a smile as she slipped the jewelry onto her left wrist.

As she stood on the elevated platform at Marcy Avenue, the wind whipping about her exposed legs, Cally found yet another reason to loathe her school uniform. Judging from the number of leers she was getting from creepy-looking guys, it was a real perv magnet.

As she walked up the stairs of the school, Cally wondered what lay ahead for her behind Bathory's blood-red doors.

The first thing she saw on entering was the full-length portrait of an outstandingly attractive woman, her milk-white face framed by reddish hair. The lilac shade of her flowing dress offset her luminous green eyes. In one slender hand she held an open roll of blank parchment; the other held a scrivener's talon.

What Cally found particularly striking was the look in the woman's eyes. Unlike other early Romantic-era paintings Cally had seen in museums, there was nothing coy or coquettish in the woman's gaze. Instead she radiated a mixture of wisdom, curiosity, and determination. She seemed to be staring expectantly at Cally, as if she had just asked a question and was patiently awaiting a reply.

Cally walked over to look at the brass plaque attached to the bottom of the portrait's frame. To her surprise, the inscription was in English, not the formal chthonic script of the Old Bloods. It read: OUR FOUNDER, MORELLA KARNSTEIN.

Even though the subject of the painting was long dead, Cally felt as if she were somehow welcoming her to the school. Maybe she could fit in here after all. But first she needed to locate the school secretary and find out what her classes would be.

Cally looked around, suddenly aware of how empty the building felt. Although there were supposed to be at least seventy students attending the school, there were no voices buzzing behind the closed doors of the classrooms or rattling of lockers in the hallways. The only sound she heard was the rapid clicking of fingernails on a computer keyboard, coming from the office on her right.

She walked in and saw a middle-aged woman dressed in a gray jacket and skirt, her long dark hair piled atop her head and held in place by several strategically placed sharpened pencils. She was seated behind a desk, entering data into a computer. On seeing Cally, the school secretary stopped, her fingers frozen in mid-keystroke.

"What are you doing aboveground?" the secretary asked sternly.

"I—I'm sorry," Cally stammered, startled by the woman's severity. "I'm a new student—I was told to report to the school secretary when I got here. . . ."

"You're the New Blood," the secretary said, her upper lip wrinkling as if she smelled something foul. "And you're late."

"I realize that," Cally said. "I had to take the subway to get here and it took longer than I thought. . . ."

"Tardiness is not tolerated at Bathory Academy. Nor is non-regulation clothing, jewelry, or accessories," the secretary said tartly as she eyed Cally's unusual hairstyle and the colorful bangles on her wrist. "While such outlandish personal fashion statements might be acceptable at a place like Varney Hall, they are frowned upon here. You would do well to remember that, Miss Monture."

"Yes, ma'am," Cally replied quietly.

The secretary got up, walked briskly to a filing cabinet, and pulled out a manila folder. She strode over to a tabletop photocopy machine and slapped a piece of paper from the folder onto the glass. Her body language made it clear that being forced to attend to a New Blood was almost too galling to bear.

"Here's your class schedule," the older woman said, literally shoving the photocopied paper into Cally's face. "You are to report immediately to the grotto for assembly. Is that understood?"

"I guess so."

"Then go join the others," she said curtly, slamming the door shut behind her.

"Thanks a lot, bitch," Cally muttered under her breath as she stood in the hallway, frowning at her class schedule.

It was printed in chthonic script, the written language of the Founders, which looked like a cross between Chinese, Sumerian, and chicken scratch. She'd learned the simplified version of the language at Varney Hall but wasn't familiar with the more formal version preferred by the Old Bloods. It was going to take a little deciphering on her part to figure out exactly when, where, and what her classes would be. To make matters worse, Cally had no clue where to find the grotto.

She looked around, desperately hoping to catch sight of a student or faculty member, but the first floor of the school was deserted, save for an undead servant dressed in janitor's grays slowly pushing a broom down the hall.

Since her family didn't have servants, Cally hadn't

grown up surrounded by the undead like most of her New Blood friends. The undead tended to creep her out. It wasn't that they scared her or anything; it was just that she didn't know where to look or what to say whenever they were around. It seemed super-weird to be waited on hand and foot by people you— or at least someone in your family—had essentially murdered.

She walked up to the caretaker sweeping the floor and politely coughed into her fist. "Excuse me . . . ?"

The janitor kept pushing his broom along the floor.

"Hello?" Cally said, a little louder than before, this time tapping him on the shoulder.

The man with the broom jumped slightly. He turned to look at her, a stunned expression on his face. "You are talking to me, mistress?" he asked, clearly baffled by why she would want to do such a thing.

"I'm sorry if I'm interrupting your work, but I was hoping you could, uh, help me find where I'm supposed to go?"

"I am only the janitor, miss."

"Yeah, I can see that. I just need to know where the grotto is."

"It is located on the third level, miss," the janitor said, turning back to his broom.

"The grotto's upstairs?" she asked with a frown, looking to the upper stories over her head.

"No, miss," the janitor replied with a shake of his head. "It is below."

"So how do I get there?"

The servant said nothing but merely pointed at a door across the hall from them marked JANITORIAL.

"But that's the supply closet," she said, frowning harder than before. She turned back to ask another question, only to find that he had already pushed his broom down the hall and around the corner.

Cally scratched her head, baffled by the janitor's instructions. Still, just to be on the safe side, she walked across the hall and peeked inside the cleaning supplies closet. Instead of a bunch of mops and cases of floor wax, she saw a large wrought-iron cage elevator complete with an undead operator dressed in a maroon jacket with Bathory Academy's insignia emblazoned across the breast pocket.

"I need to go to the grotto," she said hesitantly. The elevator operator had the same thousand-yard stare as the janitor, and it was starting to spook her.

"Very well, miss," the operator said, pulling first the interior elevator door and then the folding gate shut behind her.

Cally grabbed one of the side rails to steady herself as the car suddenly jerked into motion. "I'm new here," she explained. "Can you tell me what the grotto is?"

"I do not know, miss," the operator replied, his eyes riveted straight ahead. "I have never seen it."

Cally frowned, perplexed by his response. "You mean you work here and you don't know what the grotto actually is?"

"I am the *elevator operator*, mistress," he replied, as if that explained everything. "It is my duty to take students and faculty from one floor to the other. I have been doing so for—what year is this, mistress?"

"2008."

"*Ahhh.*" He nodded slowly. "In that case, I have been inside this elevator for one hundred and twenty-seven years. That is all I do. All I shall ever do."

"Okay. I see," Cally said, now officially creeped out. She decided to spend the rest of the lengthy ride to the mysterious grotto in silence.

Stepping out of the elevator, Cally heard a strange mixture of buzzing and high-pitched piping, as if someone had angrily shaken a hive full of bees and tossed it into a cave full of bats. She followed the sound, walking down a long vaulted corridor that ended at a huge doorway. Its massive metal doors were standing open.

As she got closer, the buzzing resolved itself into the sound of dozens upon dozens of voices talking excitedly, while the piping proved to be the ultrasonic chittering of those speaking in the true tongue, the ancient language of the Founders.

Cally stepped across the gigantic threshold and found herself not in a room but a cavern, one as grand and awe-inspiring as any cathedral. The roof soared over two hundred feet above her head, held aloft by six enormous rock pillars. If she remembered correctly what she'd learned from the tour guide during the trip she and her grandmother made to Howe Caverns when she was ten years old, the huge rock formations that hung down from the ceiling like gigantic icicles were stalactites, while those pushing up from the floor like huge fangs were stalagmites.

But as amazing as the secret grotto was, it was more amazing to see so many vampires openly gathered in one spot. Most of the vampires were in their humanoid forms, dressed in Bathory Academy or Ruthven uniforms. They sat perched, gargoyle-like, atop the various stalagmites. But there were a good number in their winged forms, clinging to the steep walls and large stalactites, hanging head down like sheaves of tobacco drying in a barn.

As she threaded her way through the maze of rock formations in search of a place to perch, those who had already claimed their spots turned to look at her, their eyes glowing in the dim light. She was keenly aware of being a new, unfamiliar face among those famous for their cliquishness.

As she tried to climb onto an unclaimed stalagmite,

a girl with red hair and emerald-green eyes jumped onto it from a nearby rock formation, hissing at Cally like a cat warding off an intruder. "This seat's taken!"

Cally wanted to tell the redhead to kiss her ass, but getting into a fight during assembly on her first day was probably not the best way to start things off. She muttered an apology and kept looking. In about a minute, she found a place to perch and quickly clambered up it.

"May I have your attention, please?"

It wasn't really a question. As the words boomed out across the cavern, the assembled students fell silent and turned in the direction of the voice. Cally followed their lead and saw a woman wearing jeweled cat's-eye glasses, with a dramatic streak of white in her raven-black hair. She was standing in the mouth of a tiny cave that hung suspended high above the floor of the grotto like a pulpit.

"For the sake of our brethren at Ruthven's, allow me to introduce myself. I am Madame Nerezza, head-mistress of Bathory Academy. Our schools are gathered here tonight to acknowledge the passing of one of our own, who was attacked by Van Helsings early Saturday morning. Her name was Tanith Graves, daughter of Dorian and Georgina Graves, and she was a third-year here at Bathory."

There was a brief flurry as the students looked at one another. Although a few gasped in surprise, the majority of the student body simply sat in silence, as quiet as the rocks on which they perched.

"My sincerest sympathies, as well as those of the combined Bathory and Ruthven faculty, are extended to Miss Graves's family and friends in this, their time of loss.

"As you all know, the Founders of our race were summoned forth over twenty thousand years ago from the infernal region, only to find themselves stranded in this dimension. Since those early days, our kind has struggled to survive in a world not our own. Yet, despite all odds, we have managed not only to endure, but to thrive. However, our success has not come without opposition—and often requires us to pay a steep price.

"If there is anything positive to be learned from this tragedy, it should be this: Van Helsings are very *real*.

"I realize this is an exciting time for you students. You are standing on the verge of adulthood and you yearn to experiment, to stretch your wings, both figuratively and literally. You hunger to embrace the night, as is your heritage. But just because you are stronger and faster than humans and possess powers that they lack, do not fool yourselves into believing you have nothing to fear from them!"

Madame Nerezza paused for a moment and looked out over the sea of young faces, then gestured with her left hand. "Look to the persons to the left of you," she commanded.

Cally found herself looking at a female student with black hair worn parted down the middle in braided double pigtails fixed by red ribbons.

"Now look to your right," the headmistress instructed.

All heads dutifully turned again—save for the girl to Cally's right. Instead of looking at the back of her neighbor's head, Cally found herself looking directly into the face of the blonde she had challenged at the park. Judging by the expression of sheer, unalloyed hatred shining in her eyes like blue steel blades, the blonde recognized Cally too.

"The cold, hard truth of the matter is that within a hundred years, one of the three of you will be dead," Madame Nerezza intoned. "Such is life for our kind. And it is the duty of our schools to prepare you for it."

Cally swallowed hard, quickly looking away from the blonde's searing gaze. Something told her she wouldn't have to wait a hundred years to find out if the headmistress's prediction was accurate.

CHAPTER 10

As everyone started leaving, Lilith hopped down from her perch and began searching the students filing out of the grotto, hoping to catch sight of Jules. She needed to find him before he returned to Ruthven's so she could tell him she had just spotted the New Blood from the park.

As she wound through a stand of stalagmites, she heard Jules's voice coming from up ahead. Rounding a cone-shaped rock, she spotted him standing next to one of the great columns that supported the roof of the grotto, looking up toward the ceiling.

"Praise the Founders I found you," she said as she hurried toward him.

"Hi there, Lili," he said, turning to greet her. "I was just talking to my cousin," he explained, pointing upward.

Lilith raised her eyes and found herself staring up

at Xander Orlock. Jules's cousin was clinging to the side of the column like a lizard on a garden wall.

"Uh, yeah. Hi, Exo," Lilith said, fighting back a grimace as she looked into his face.

Unlike the majority of students who attended Ruthven's and Bathory, Xander did not use any kind of artificial tanning agent on his skin. His complexion was so pale it was actually translucent, giving him a slightly bluish cast. With his large, protruding eyes, unnaturally long fingers, and pointed ear tips, Lilith found it difficult to believe that Xander was in any way related to Jules.

"Hello, Lilith," Xander said with just the faintest lisp. Due to inbreeding on his father's side of the family, he had a hard time fully retracting his fangs, which sometimes affected his speech.

"Remember that newbie bitch that nearly got us killed the other night?" Lilith asked Jules.

"The one from the park?" Jules frowned. "What about her?"

"She's here in the grotto!"

"There's a newbie at Bathory?" Xander asked. "How is that even possible?"

"I don't know," Lilith growled in disgust. "Maybe she's not a New Blood after all. Either that or Nerezza's hard up for tuition fees."

"Are you sure it's her?" Jules asked.

"Yes, I'm sure! I'll *never* forget her face for as long as

I live!" Lilith snapped. "She was sitting right next to me during assembly. I would have killed her right then if the headmistress wasn't there!"

"Look, Lilith, there's no point doing something rash," Jules said. "You know that schools are vendetta-free zones. If you try and do anything within a mile of here, you won't just be expelled, they'll haul you before the Synod and try you as a criminal."

"I've never seen an actual New Blood before." Xander grinned. "Maybe I'll hang around and check her out!"

"Shut up, Exo!" Lilith snapped, no longer able to hide her irritation with his presence. "No one's talking to you!"

"Okay. I know when I'm not wanted." Xander sighed. He quickly reversed his grip on the column's surface and scurried back into the shadows.

"*Ugh!* I don't know why you let that spod hang around you," Lilith said with a shudder.

"I admit, he's kinda spoddy, but he's an okay guy, and it's not like he gets much of a chance to meet hot chicks on his own." Jules laughed. "Exo's been hanging around me since we were little. You didn't have to yell at him."

"I could care less about Exo getting a date," Lilith said peevishly. "I want to know what that newbie bitch is trying to pull. First she shows up at the park just before the Van Helsings attack, and now she's here! I don't like her, Jules. There's something not right about her. I sensed it the moment I laid eyes on her. What if she's a stalking horse in cahoots with the Van Helsings?"

"Lilith, the Van Helsings were trying to kill her too." Jules sighed. "I was there, remember? In fact, if she hadn't taken out that Van Helsing, you'd probably be as dead as Tanith right now."

"Why are you sticking up for her?" Lilith snapped, her eyes flashing blue fire. "Are you saying you wish I was dead?"

"That's biting below the belt, Lilith," Jules replied, stung by her response. "I'm just saying that maybe you should take it easy. I don't want to see you get hurt. . . ."

"Oh, now you think I'm no match for her, is that it?" Lilith said tartly.

"All right, you two lovebirds, break it up," Coach Knorrig said as she walked up to them. "Todd, hit the locker room and get dressed for shapeshifting. And I want *you*, Mr. Heartthrob"—she pointed a finger at Jules—"to get your ass back to Ruthven's. *Pronto.*"

"Yes, coach," Jules said, secretly relieved to escape.

As he jogged off in the direction of the tunnel that connected the grotto with Ruthven's School for Boys, Jules tried not to think about the weird look in Lilith's eyes as she talked about the New Blood. He knew how obsessive Lilith could be. He hoped she would get over whatever was eating her and start acting like she used to. That's all any of them wanted, really: for things to go back to how they were before the park. Certainly that wasn't too much to ask?

Cally stood in a large clearing in the center of the grotto, staring up at the towering columns of living rock that supported the cathedral-like roof. "I never knew there were caves like this under Manhattan," she whispered in amazement.

"There aren't."

She turned around to find the girl she'd seen earlier, the one with the braided pigtails, standing behind her—except now there were two of her, one wearing red ribbons in her hair, the other wearing blue. Cally blinked to make sure her eyes weren't playing tricks on her, but the duplicate didn't disappear.

"They mean *none* of this is real," a girl with turquoise beads in her hair said, "at least not the way *you* think it is. This isn't a natural cave—it was carved out of the rock by hand. Everything you see here was artificially created during the mid-nineteenth century."

"People actually *built* this?" Cally said in disbelief. She looked around again, and this time she noticed there was indeed a pattern to the stalagmites and stalactites in their sizes, shapes, and positions. The same was true of the huge columns, which she could now see were exactly equidistant from one another.

"Sort of. They used undead labor. It took over thirty

years for them to dig this place out, working twenty-four/seven. It was designed so we could learn to fly down here."

"Pretty damn impressive for a gym," Cally said with a chuckle. "Thanks for the info. My name's Cally Monture, by the way."

"I'm Melinda Mauvais. And the tag team over there's Bella and Bette Maledetto."

"I'm Bella," said the twin with the blue ribbons.

"Bette," said the twin with the red ribbons.

"Nice to meet you all."

"I like your bangles," Melinda said. "Where'd you get them?"

"These?" Cally held up her left arm and rattled the bangles on her wrist. "My grandmother gave them to me before she, uh, before she left for Europe."

"Have we met before somewhere?" Melinda asked, cocking her head to one side as she eyed the new girl's haircut. "Do you hang out at the Belfry?"

"Afraid not," Cally replied with a shake of her head. "Is that some kind of club?"

"Over on West Twentieth."

"Oh," Cally said, "I normally do my clubbing farther downtown—you know, SoHo, Tribeca. . . ."

"Maybe *that's* where I've seen you," Melinda decided. "I'm down around SoHo and Tribeca quite a bit."

"Melly!"

Melinda turned to see Lilith bearing down on her.

Before she could respond, Lilith grabbed her by the upper arm and steered her away from Cally.

"*What do you think you're doing?*" Lilith hissed at her friend.

"Just talking to the new girl, that's all," Melinda replied, bewildered by Lilith's anger. "What's up with you?"

"Don't you *know* who that is?"

"She said her name was Cally something. . . ."

"She's the New Blood from the park and she's the reason Tanith's dead!" Lilith snapped.

Melinda frowned. "I *thought* she looked familiar! But what's a New Blood doing here?"

"I don't know. But what I *do* know is I don't want you talking to her. You know, Melly," Lilith growled, "I've overlooked the fact that you're friendly with those half-blood Maledettos, even though you know *their* father is *my* father's sworn enemy. But being friendly with a New Blood—especially *this* one—is another thing altogether! I would *hate* to have something like this get in the way of our friendship. Understood?"

"Perfectly." Melinda winced as Lilith's grip tightened on her arm.

"Who's the nutcase?" Cally asked, pointing to the girl with the long hair who had just dragged Melinda away.

"That's Lilith Todd," Bella responded.

"Todd? As in *Victor* Todd?" Cally gasped, her eyes widening in surprise.

"He's her father," Bette said.

"Okay, ladies! Enough chitchat!" Knorrig shouted, clapping her hands together. "I want those of you who are *supposed* to be down here in that locker room and dressed for class in five minutes! That means *you*, Mauvais! And you too, Maledetto! No, not you, the *other* Maledetto! Don't make me tell you a *third* time, Todd! I mean it! The rest of you, get back to whatever class you're supposed to be in! Just because we had an assembly this evening doesn't mean you're free to blow off first period!"

"Excuse me," Cally said, looking down at her class schedule, then back up at the woman dressed in gray sweats and a pair of black Chuck Taylors, a whistle dangling around her neck and a Yankees cap pulled down low on her head. "Are you Coach, uh, Knorrig?"

"I'm not your fairy godmother, that's for goddamn sure. Yeah, I'm Knorrig. You must be the new girl."

"Yes, ma'am. I'm Cally Monture."

"Come with me, Monture," Knorrig said, leading her out of the cavern and back down the tunnel to her office. "I've got some shifting wear for you."

"Shifting wear?" Cally's belly fluttered like a curtain in a strong breeze. "Is this a shapeshifting class?"

"Of course," Coach Knorrig replied, shooting the new student a curious look as she opened a cabinet and pulled out a short-sleeved red terry-cloth one-piece with a zip-up front. "What the hell else do you think we'd be teaching down here? Square dancing? Yoga? Here you go, Monture. Wear it in good health."

"Are you *serious*?" Cally gasped, holding the garment up by its sleeves.

"I'll admit it's not the sexiest thing on the face of the earth, but it *has* been charmed to change along with you so you're not running around naked out there. And that's what matters, as far as I'm concerned. Now go get changed. Oh—and make sure you take those things off your wrist," Coach Knorrig said, nodding at the bangles Cally was wearing. "You don't want them getting broken when you change."

As Cally left Coach Knorrig's office, the door to the locker room across the hall opened and a group of students emerged, Lilith Todd at their head. As they passed each other in the hallway, Lilith stared at Cally, her eyes shining like gun barrels, then she jostled the new girl hard enough to make her drop the gym suit. When Cally stooped to pick up her shifting wear, the redhead who had challenged her earlier stepped on her hand, pinching her fingers.

"*Owww!*" Cally yelped, yanking her hand out from under the other girl's foot. "Watch it!"

"Oopsie!" the redhead said, flashing Cally a snide smile. "I'm *sooo* sorry! I didn't see you there, what with you being *beneath* me."

The other girls burst into derisive laughter. As the group made their way down the corridor, Lilith glanced back over her shoulder with a look as black and cold as ice on a highway.

Changing into the gym suit, Cally shook her head in mock dismay: barely an hour into her first day at school and she was already on the shit list of the daughter of one of the most well-known Old Bloods in the world.

As she hurried from the locker room to join the rest of the class, she told herself that focusing on the negative wasn't going to get her anywhere she wanted to be. Sure, Lilith was down on her. Cally couldn't really blame her, after what happened at the park. But that didn't mean things had to stay ugly between them.

The way she saw it, she had two choices: either she could put up with their bitchiness and bullying like a dog taking a beating, or she could take the initiative and try to work things out between her and Lilith. Still, it was difficult to feel poised and self-confident while her gym suit was working its way up her butt crack.

"Gather round, girls," Coach Knorrig said, motioning with her clipboard. "Tonight we're going for speed." She held up a stopwatch. "Being able to shapeshift quickly while you're on the move is a must. If you're being chased by Van Helsings, for example, you can't waste valuable time going from one form to another. Your transformation should be as easy as tossing on a coat. Having to come to a dead stop in order to shape-shift will leave you exactly that—dead. Who wants to go first?"

The students glanced around uneasily. No one raised a hand.

"Okay, if that's how it's going to be, then I guess you're it, Mauvais. The rest of you, give her some room."

Melinda stepped forward, frowning as she fingered the beads woven through her hair. "Do I *have* to, Coach?"

"Did I *not* tell you not to wear your hair braided like that when we have shifting? It's not *my* fault you don't pay attention, Mauvais."

Melinda sighed in resignation while the other girls in the class formed a semicircle around her.

"You ready?" Coach Knorrig asked, her thumb on the stopwatch's timer button. Melinda nodded. "Go!"

Melinda's eyes rolled back in her head, revealing their whites, as her body began to spasm like a landed fish. There was a wet popping sound as the bones in her body dislocated themselves and began to slide about underneath her skin. The palms of her hands darkened and swelled into pads, and retractable claws sprang from her nail beds. As Melinda threw her head back and opened her mouth as far as it could go, huge yellow fangs slid from her gums. Her ears grew longer and pointier as they migrated to the top of her head, and the roar of a big cat sprang from her throat.

There was a sound like someone hitting a bag of half-rotten oranges with a baseball bat and her nose and brow ridge abruptly bowed outward, as if something was trying to punch its way out from inside her skull. She pulled her lips back in a snarl as the bridge of her nose elongated and widened itself. Whiskers shot out from her muzzle. At the same time the hair atop her head writhed with a life of its own, sending the beadwork shooting out in every direction. Her hair spread down her spine and across her shoulders like a fast-growing vine until it covered her entire body. Finally, no longer able to stand upright, she dropped onto all fours, a deep, guttural sound halfway between a purr and a growl rumbling in her transformed chest.

"And—time!" Coach Knorrig called as she hit the stop button. "Twenty-eight point five-seven seconds." She pulled a ballpoint pen out from behind her ear and jotted down something on the clipboard.

What crouched in the center of the semicircle was not exactly a panther but more of an approximation of such a beast. At first glance it looked like a jungle cat, but as Cally looked closer, she could see that the snarling animal not only lacked a tail, it also had thumbs in place of dewclaws.

"Was my time good?" Melinda asked hopefully

when she'd morphed back into her humanoid form.

"Not bad, but you need to do better," Coach Knorrig replied. "Now pick up the beads."

"It's going to take me forever to get these things woven back in!" Melinda moaned as she knelt to pick up the scattered pieces of turquoise.

"Cry me a river, Mauvais," Coach Knorrig growled. "Maybe next time you'll listen to me when I tell you not to do something. Okay, Monture: you're next."

"Huh? Who? Me?" Cally gazed around, a confused look on her face.

"Yes, you. Go take your place."

"I-I don't know if I can do this, Coach—"

"Of *course* you can!" The coach scowled. "It's just a matter of wanting it."

"No, that's not what I meant," Cally replied, her cheeks turning red. "It's just that at my old school, shifting was a fourth-year subject."

"Really? That late?" Coach Knorrig frowned. "Where did you go to school?" she asked, flipping through the papers on her clipboard. "Académie Cauchemar in Paris? The Glamis School in Scotland?"

"Varney Hall."

"*What!*" Coach Knorrig nearly dropped her clipboard. "The headmistress didn't say you were a New Blood." She motioned to Cally, who took a cautious step forward. "Look, kid, this is an intermediary class. All the other girls passed introductory shapeshifting last year. Until I talk with the headmistress and find out what is going on here, I don't want you working out with the rest of the class. The last thing you need is to end up crippled for life because you can't turn your shank back into a shin or retract your finger bones properly—assuming you're capable of shapeshifting in the first place."

"Does this mean I'm excused from class?" Cally asked hopefully.

"You wish." Coach Knorrig snorted. "It means you're running laps. Starting now."

As Cally passed the stalagmite shaped like a melted Statue of Liberty for the twenty-fifth time, a dark figure separated itself from the shadows above her head and swooped down, its black wings spread wide and its fang-filled mouth yawning open.

Seconds before the creature touched down, it shimmered like a desert mirage and Coach Knorrig stood before her, still dressed in her sweats. "That's enough for tonight, Monture. Go hit the showers."

"That was amazing, Coach." Cally gasped as she caught her breath. "I didn't even see you change."

"That's the whole point, kiddo. Everyone starts out slow, but once you learn the ropes, you can pull it off in the blink of an eye. I spoke to Madame Nerezza about your situation. I need to have an idea of what you can and can't do physically. You're to report down here after school tonight so I can work up a proper assessment of your abilities."

"Sure, Coach. Thanks."

"Oh, by the way, Monture—why didn't you correct me when I called you a New Blood?"

"Beg pardon?" Cally asked, uncertain as to what the older woman meant.

"Nerezza says you're here on a legacy grant," the coach said meaningfully. When Cally didn't respond, Knorrig sighed and shook her head. "That makes you Old Blood, Monture," she explained.

"Only on one side, ma'am," Cally said quietly.

"Oh!" the coach exclaimed, her eyes widening slightly. "So you're a half-blood, eh? Well, the Maledetto twins have a New Blood parent, and they're among my better students."

As she made her way back to the locker room, Cally spotted Lilith Todd walking by herself. Seeing her chance, Cally hurried to catch up.

"Lilith—?"

The blonde turned around, but the moment she saw Cally, her features became hard and her blue eyes flashed pure, undiluted hate. "What do you want, newbie?" she snarled.

"Just to talk, that's all," Cally replied. "Look, I realize we didn't get off on the best foot the other night. I got carried away, but I didn't really mean anything by it, honest. And I'm sorry about your friend. I mean that. But there's no point in there being bad blood between us now that we're attending school together. So what do you say?" she asked as she extended an open hand to Lilith. "No hard feelings?"

Lilith glowered as if Cally's hand were full of fresh manure. "I don't know what kind of game you're trying to play with me, bitch—but I'm not falling for it."

"Game? What game?" Cally asked. Despite her original desire to mend fences, she could feel herself getting mad. "I'm just trying to be nice here. . . ."

"*Nice* is for losers, Monture." Lilith's face was contorted in disgust. "It beats me how you managed to talk Madame Nerezza into allowing you into Bathory in the first place, but staying around is only going to make things hard on you. *Very* hard.

"You got off easy the other night because you caught me by surprise with that stormgathering trick of yours. I won't let you do that again. If you know what's good for you, you'll leave this school right this minute and stay clear of me for the rest of your miserable, so-called life. Because if I ever run across you again in your lowlife hipster gear—anywhere outside of this lousy school—I swear I'll kill you."

"Is that a threat, Todd?"

"It's a *prediction*, Monture," Lilith replied coldly.

"And another thing: stay away from my friends! The next time I catch you so much as *looking* at one of them, I'll rip your eyes out of their sockets and feed them to you."

CHAPTER 11

Scrivening was Cally's last class of the night. She eyed the double row of antique lift-top desks with built-in inkwells. She knew she'd miss her friends, but she didn't expect to miss Varney's modern feel. Bathory was so retro it was like walking into a time warp, right down to the sputtering gaslight fixtures that were the only light in the winding subterranean halls.

As Cally moved to take a seat at the front of the room, Carmen Duivel stepped around her and quickly sat down at the desk.

"This is *my* seat, newbie." Carmen smirked. "I always sit here."

Cally sighed and moved to the next desk over, only to have Melinda Mauvais block her attempt to sit down.

"Sorry," Melinda said, trying not to look at Cally's

face as she spoke. "This seat's taken."

Cally had already experienced this childish strategy in both her beast mastery and mesmerism classes. She took a seat in the back of the class and hoped the instructor wouldn't spend the entire period staring at her like she was some kind of repulsive bug.

"Young ladies, please open your desks and remove your scrivening kits," Madame Geraint announced as she stepped in front of the blackboard. The scrivening instructor was a thin woman with exceptionally well-formed hands. Her fingers moved with an otherworldly grace, like seaweed floating in a gentle current.

Cally opened the top of her desk and found a black lacquer stationery box. Its lid was decorated with a mother-of-pearl inlay depicting the Bathory Academy seal: a capital Gothic script *B* framed by wolfsbane and deadly nightshade. Inside, the box held several sheets of vellum parchment, a flat stone paperweight, and a six-inch scrivener's talon fashioned of ebony.

Madame Geraint used a wooden pointer and tapped a chart showing what looked like a cross between a Chinese ideogram and a line drawing by a drunken Picasso.

"Tonight you will be practicing how to properly write the chthonic word for *blood*. In the true tongue it would be called thusly." She cleared her throat, then issued a rapid series of ultra-high-frequency clicks and chirps. "Note the accent on the last syllable.

Depending on the context, the word for blood can be used to describe life, food, or family, making it the most important word in our vocabulary. Talons up, ladies! And—commence!"

Cally removed a sheet of vellum from the stationery box, carefully placing the paperweight at the bottom of the page. Luckily, she had taken scrivening at Varney, so she wasn't completely lost. Still, mastering a scrivener's talon was difficult even for an Old Blood, so she had to pay extra attention to what she was doing at all times.

She picked up the talon, using her thumb to hold it correctly against her right index finger, which she then bent to match the curvature of the instrument, and dipped the talon's nib in the glass jar of ink set within the inkwell. Cally carefully tapped off the excess ink before placing the nib onto the parchment.

"No, no, no! This is utter guano! Start again with a fresh sheet!"

The class raised its collective head to see who was being reprimanded. Madame Geraint was standing over Carmen Duivel's desk, shaking her head in disapproval.

"Who cares if it's not perfect?" Carmen retorted, her cheeks red with embarrassment for being singled out. "If I want to write anything, I can just type it on my computer. That way if I make any mistakes, I just hit delete instead of having to start a whole new page. Writing this way is stupid, if you ask me."

A nervous titter ran through the rest of the class.

"Computers!" Madame Geraint snorted derisively. "Keyboards have ruined your generation's ability to hold a talon properly, much less write legibly. Of course, in the earliest days, there was no need for such things as writing instruments. Our ancestors simply dipped their claw tips in ink and wrote directly onto parchment scrolls.

"While we have embraced such technological advances as the printing press and have even developed software that allows us to communicate with one another via the internet, our most important documents are *still* generated by hand. Let me assure you that the ability to read and write chthonic script is far from 'stupid.' In all the legal documents, religious writings, and genealogical data generated by our people over the millennia, not one word has ever been penned in a language known to humans. *This* is how we protect ourselves from those who would eradicate us from the face of the earth.

"Skilled scriveners are highly prized by the Synod's law keepers, and scrivening plays a major role in electing the Lord Chancellor and other high officials."

"Well, that's nothing I have to worry about." Carmen sniffed. "I have no plans on being a civil servant when I graduate."

"That may very well be, Miss Duivel," Madame Geraint said with a sigh. "But seeing as your mother is the one paying your tuition, it is my job to make sure you do not leave this school a functional illiterate. Now start again."

Carmen scowled but dared not say anything else as she restarted her copying. Madame Geraint watched over her shoulder for a couple of moments before resuming her silent patrol of the classroom, her strangely elegant hands clasped behind her back.

As the bell signaling the end of the school night sounded, Madame Geraint pointed to the front of the room. "Young ladies, please put away your scrivening kits, sign your work sheets, and leave them for me on my desk."

Cally quickly replaced her scrivening instruments and gathered up her work sheet. As she approached the line of students waiting to drop off their work, Samara Bleak turned to fix her with a withering glare.

"Back of the line, newbie."

"But there are other people behind me . . ." Cally protested.

"You heard her, bitch. She said 'back of the line,'" Carmen snarled, giving Cally's shoulder a sharp shove.

Cally staggered backward, her thigh striking one of the desks.

"You having any trouble, Carmen?" Melinda asked, glaring at Cally.

"No problem. I'm just teaching this newbie her place, that's all."

Cally wanted more than anything to punch her in the mouth, but that was exactly what they *wanted* her to do. She clenched her fists so tightly the fingernails drew blood from her palms. As much as she loved the idea of grinding Carmen's evil Kewpie-doll face under her heel, she had to restrain herself.

If it was up to her, she would blow off Coach Knorrig and the stupid assessment and walk out the front door and never come back. But doing that meant completely destabilizing her living arrangements, not to mention Sheila. Despite her weaknesses and failings, Sheila was still her mother and it was up to Cally to protect her as best she could. And if that meant having to eat the oldies' shit, then so be it.

As she placed her work sheet atop the others stacked on the desk, Madame Geraint stepped forward, placing her hand on Cally's own. Although the teacher's fingers looked as fragile as stalks of new grass, they were surprisingly supple and strong.

"May I see that, please?" Madame Geraint asked as she picked up Cally's work sheet. She held the page at arm's length, studying it with an intent look on her face, then glanced down at Cally. "It would seem you possess a dab-hand."

"Is that a good thing?"

"Yes, child, it is," Madame Geraint said, smiling with one side of her mouth. "It means your work shows power and control, as well as a certain refinement. I could tell you had talent while I was supervising the class but did not consider it wise to call attention to you in front of the others."

"Thank you, ma'am—I guess."

"I'm certain you are aware there are instructors who resent your being enrolled at Bathory, Miss Monture. I am not one of them. I find such snobbery grossly hypocritical." Madame Geraint sniffed. "After all, instructors are invariably the last of usurped bloodlines. It's like the old saying: 'Those who can become New Bloods; those who can't teach.'"

Cally changed into her gym suit and stood waiting for her assessment.

"Learning about the history of our kind and how to scriven is all well and good. But if you don't master the ability to shapeshift and fly, you'll never live to see your centenary," Coach Knorrig stated as she paced back and forth.

"While shapeshifting is an ability all of us possess, it is not something you just fall out of bed knowing how to do. When you get right down to it, it's all a question of muscle memory. In order to maximize muscle memory, you have to repeat the transformation process over and over again until it becomes automatic. That means practice, practice, and still more practice.

"I'm not gonna to lie to you—shapeshifting *hurts*, especially when you're new to it. Luckily, the more you do it, the easier it becomes. However, it is highly dangerous to attempt to shapeshift before you know what you're changing into. Depending on your lineage, it could be any number of things."

She finally got to the point.

"We need to figure out your totem animal first and work from there. Maybe it's a wolf. Or it could be a big cat, like Mauvais. Although it's not very likely, you might even be one of the rare ones who turns into a king cobra or some other kind of snake. We'll just have to see. Okay, Monture, just do what I tell you, okay? First I want you to close your eyes and clear your mind."

Cally closed her eyes and tried to relax, taking in a deep breath through her nose and drawing it into her belly.

"That's good. Very good. Now I want you to reach down deep, deep inside your mind," Coach Knorrig said, her voice taking the tone of a mother urging her child into sleep. "Go down into the darkness. Tell me: what do you see?"

Cally was about to tell Coach Knorrig all she saw was a bunch of purplish blots pulsating behind her eyelids when she realized she was looking at a dense cluster of trees and underbrush.

"I-I see a forest," she stammered.

"Good. Very, very good," the coach said encouragingly. "What greets you in the forest?"

Cally's brow furrowed as she concentrated harder, trying to bring the forest behind her eyes into sharper detail. As she moved farther into the edge of the woods, a pair of eyes as red as live coals suddenly blinked into existence in the oil-black darkness between the trunks of the gnarled trees. There was a low growling sound and a gray timber wolf stepped out of the shadows, sniffing the air cautiously.

"I see a wolf," she said excitedly.

"Excellent," Coach Knorrig said. "That is your totem, the beast of your family line. It is as much a part of your heritage as the color of your eyes and hair. I want you to try to touch it."

Cally nodded and took a tentative step forward as she raised her right hand. The wolf sniffed her as it moved toward her in a series of cautious half steps, as if uncertain whether to attack or flee.

"Can you see its energy?"

Although she had not noticed it at first, Cally could now see that the timber wolf was bathed in a strange, greenish glow.

"Yes," she said, nodding.

"Good, good. Place your hand on the wolf and let its energy flow into you."

Cally reached out and cautiously stroked the wolf's fur, running her hand along its spine. Even though she knew there was nothing in front of her but empty air, she could feel the warmth of its body underneath her hand and feel its soft fur between her fingers. Petting the creature triggered an unexpected sense of well-being within her, as if she had returned home after a long trip to find a fire crackling in the hearth and her loved ones gathered to greet her.

The greenish fire that surrounded the wolf wrapped itself around her hand, traveling up her arm like a quick-growing vine. But as it reached her shoulder, she was suddenly gripped by searing pain, as if someone was breaking her bones from the inside out.

Coach Knorrig watched intently as Cally dropped to her knees, grimacing in agony as her right arm began to swell and contort into the foreleg of a wolf.

"C'mon, Monture—you're doing great! Don't be afraid. Take the wolf's power and make it your own!"

Fearful that the animal would slip free of her grip, Cally dug her fingers deep into its fur, only to have the beast turn and snap at her with its fearsome jaws. Even though she knew what she was seeing was not real in the physical sense, she instinctively pulled away as the animal lunged at her. The wolf promptly turned and bounded off into the shadows between the trees, taking with it her sense of well-being.

"No! Wait! Don't go!" Cally cried out, reaching out as if to summon the creature back.

The smell of ozone filled the air and Coach Knorrig gasped in shock to find her student's outstretched arm sheathed in dark energy. The ectoplasm was as black as spilled oil and laced with traceries of scarlet that seemed to pulse like veins and arteries. As Coach Knorrig watched in amazement, black ectoplasm began to drip from the schoolgirl's straining fingertips, sizzling as it struck the cold stone floor of the grotto like beads of water on a hot skillet.

"Open your eyes!" Coach Knorrig yelled. "Monture, open your eyes!"

The moment Cally's eyes flew open, the black ectoplasm disappeared, reabsorbed into her body. Her arm dropped limply to her side as she looked around at her surroundings, slightly dazed.

"I'm sorry, Coach," she said. "The wolf ran away. Do you want me to try again?"

"That's okay, Monture," Coach Knorrig replied as she scribbled notes on her clipboard. "I think I've seen enough."

CHAPTER 12

It was very late by the time Cally started home. As if having to deal with students who hated her guts and faculty who thought she was trash wasn't bad enough, the commute to and from her new school was a bitch and a half.

She stood on the platform in Williamsburg for a long moment and stared after the taillights of the departing J train. She looked around, hoping to catch sight of Peter, then shook her head, chiding herself for being so stupid. Getting involved with a Van Helsing was the last thing she needed. It made as much sense as a mongoose falling for a cobra or a mermaid longing for a fisherman. Nothing good could possibly come of it.

Cally could still remember when she was four years old and fell off the top of the jungle gym at the playground and broke her arm. She had cried for a minute, more in surprise than from the pain, then jumped up and started playing again as if nothing had happened.

Her grandmother, who was watching from the sidelines, quickly hurried Cally away, explaining to the other adults that she was rushing her grandchild to the nearest emergency room. Instead of going to the hospital, they took a cab back home, where Granny sat her down at the kitchen table and explained the differences between Cally and other children.

"You have to be careful when you're playing with humans, little one," her grandmother said. "They look the same as you, but they're very different. When they fall down and hurt themselves, humans can't get better right away like you do. You have to understand this. If you hurt yourself in public, you can *never* let them see you get better. You have to pretend you're still hurt and get away as fast as you can.

"If the humans find out what you are, they'll take you away from me and your mother. No matter how nice they seem, it's very, very important that you *never* reveal what you really are to anyone, especially to humans."

Her grandmother's warning still ringing in her ears, Cally slung her Diesel book bag over her shoulder and headed down the metal stairs that led to the streets below. Even though it was late, she needed to pick up a few things for herself and her mom before returning to the apartment. On reaching the bottom of the stairway, she jogged across the street and into the all-night market on the corner.

She grabbed one of the shopping baskets stacked just inside the door and set about finding what she needed: toilet paper, fingernail polish, a box of cupcakes, a bottle of Yoo-hoo, and, lastly, a bouquet of fresh-cut flowers. As he packed her things, the cashier eyed her school blazer, pleated skirt, and penny loafers with open interest.

"So—are you just dressed up like a naughty Catholic schoolgirl or are you the real thing?" He grinned salaciously.

"Get bent, sicko," Cally said, flipping him off as she snatched up the plastic grocery bag and marched out the door, swinging the bouquet of flowers in one hand. Cally had just one more errand to run before she could return home for the night.

Surrounded on all sides by businesses and apartment buildings, Rest Haven Cemetery had originally been laid out in the 1830s. A wrought-iron gate, its top lined with forbidding metal spikes, allowed passersby a brief glimpse of the cool green lawns, shade trees, and weather-worn monuments on the other side. Heavy-duty chains were wrapped about the locked gate like a chrome python, protecting the dead behind its walls from vandals, drunks, and junkies looking for a place to sleep it off.

After checking up and down the street to make sure she wasn't being watched, Cally took a running jump, landing solidly atop the wall. She paused for a second to make sure nothing had fallen out of her grocery bag before dropping to the grass on the other side.

She had always loved how Rest Haven seemed to be so far removed from the grime and noise of the city. With its birds, squirrels, and old oak trees, the half acre reminded her more of Granny's summer cabin in the country than a graveyard.

She silently wound her way through the moonlit headstones to the graves of her grandparents, which were covered by a blanket of scarlet leaves from a nearby hawthorn tree. Their granite headstone was shaped like two hearts linked by a descending dove.

Although the name on the left-hand side of the monument had undergone two decades of exposure to the elements, it was still perfectly legible: CYRIL MONTURE, 1925–1988. The inscription on the other side was far more recent: SINA OSTERBERG MONTURE, 1931–2006.

"Hi, Granny; hi, Grandpa. I brought you some new flowers," Cally said as she removed the withered snapdragons from the memorial vase and put in the fresh bouquet.

As she swept the leaves from her grandmother's

grave with her hand, she caught a familiar scent on the wind. Cally looked over her shoulder at a large monument carved in the shape of a weeping angel collapsed in grief over the bier of a loved one.

"Why are you here? Who's with you?" she asked.

A shadow separated itself from one of the angel's wings and stepped into the dim light reflected from the street. "There's no need to be scared," Peter Van Helsing said, reaching toward her. "I'm here alone."

"This is getting ridiculous!" Cally unexpectedly found herself wanting to cry. "It was weird enough that you tracked me to the club—but how could you have known I would be here, of all places?"

"What can I say? I was raised to be a stalker." He shrugged apologetically. "You were so upset last night, you left before I could explain things to you. I don't want to see you hurt, Cally Monture."

"That's funny—you were trying to kill me when we first met." She snorted. "Wait a minute—I never told you my last name."

"I know a lot about you and your family, Cally."

"Why should I believe a word you say?"

"I realize you have every reason not to trust me. But maybe you'll believe your own eyes." Peter reached inside his jacket pocket and took out an old photograph, its edges slightly foxed with age. "I slipped this out of one of my father's files. If he knew I had it, he'd kick my ass. It's a picture of your grandmother with my father, Christopher Van Helsing, and his then-protégé, Ike Grainger."

Cally stared in stunned disbelief at the picture Peter handed her. The woman looking out at her was younger than she could remember her grandmother ever being, but there was no mistaking her smile and the gleam in her eyes. She was standing in between a tall, handsome man with wavy, auburn hair not unlike Peter's and a heavyset African American youth who she recognized as the older vampire hunter she'd fried in the park.

"When was this taken?"

"About thirty years ago," Peter replied. "Not long after my father took over the Institute from my grandfather."

"I still don't understand," Cally said in a puzzled voice. "What was Granny doing with your father?"

"Don't you see? She was one of the Elites—those who are trained to use the supernatural in order to hunt vampires. According to my father, Sina was one of the best."

"This has to be bogus!" Cally said hotly, shoving the picture back into his hands. "I bet you Photoshopped it! You're crazy! My grandmother wasn't a vampire hunter—"

"Your grandmother was a *witch*, Cally," Peter said firmly, grabbing her wrist. "She was a white witch who used her powers to fight for the greater good, but she was a witch nonetheless. More importantly, she was a human. As is your mother."

"That's it—I'm not going to listen to any more of this garbage!" Cally snapped as she picked up the sack of groceries at her feet. "You are insane, do you know that? Now leave me alone!"

"No! I'm not letting you go until you listen to me!" Peter said, pushing her back so that he pinned her against the hawthorn tree. The grocery sack fell to the ground, its contents spilling across a nearby grave.

Although she could have easily broken free of his grip, Cally couldn't bring herself to. She stared up into Peter's face. She could feel his breath on her cheek as the ripe, warm smell of him filled her senses. She looked up into his eyes and saw herself reflected in them, as if she was somehow trapped inside his head.

"Why are you doing this?" she asked.

"Because I want to help you."

She gave a bitter laugh. "Since when do Van Helsings want to help vampires?"

"Because you're *not* a vampire, Cally. No vampire would have sicced a rat on a human and then turned around and tried to save him the way you did. And since when do vampires eat junk food?" He pointed to the snack cakes lying on the ground. "How long have you been trying to pass, Cally? Six months? A year?"

Cally's first instinct was to lie to Peter as she had lied to every other human in her life. From that day she'd fallen in the playground, her grandmother had drummed into her that she must never tell the truth about herself to others, no matter what. Lying was a reflex action. She opened her mouth to deny his accusations but found herself saying:

"Almost two years."

Cally was shocked by how good it felt to actually admit the truth. Since her grandmother's death, she hadn't been able to truly talk to anyone, but she dared to try to tell Peter.

"The junk food's for my mom, not me. I started metabolizing blood three years ago. Granny began weaning me off solid food after she found out about her cancer. She knew I could drink only blood if I was going to pass for one of them after she died."

Cally gripped his hand more tightly. "I won't lie to you, Peter—sometimes I get so tired of pretending to be something that I'm not, I want to just chuck it all."

"You don't *have* to keep living a lie, Cally. You can come with me to the Institute. I'll see to it that your mother's properly taken care of. You won't have to worry about looking after her anymore."

"You want me to become a Van Helsing?" Cally was shocked. "I could never do something like that!"

"You're a hybrid, Cally. How long do you think you can continue passing for a true-born now that you're at Bathory Academy? They're bound to find out the truth about your parentage sooner or later."

"How do you know about the school?" she gasped.

"Come on; give me *some* credit, will you?" Peter smiled crookedly. "I know the uniform when I see it. My ancestor burned down the original school, after all. You don't have to worry about accidentally betraying its location to me. The Institute's known about it for decades. Besides, it's too heavily fortified now for us to try anything like that again . . . not to mention it's really hard to explain driving stakes through the hearts of teenage girls to the police."

She looked over her shoulder at her grandmother's gravestone, gleaming like a diadem in the pale moonlight. "But if what you say about my grandmother is true, she had her reasons for keeping me away from the Institute. As much as I want to be with you—I can't do what you're asking of me."

Peter took a deep breath and let it out again. "I suspected that would be your answer." He handed her a card. "Here, take my number. If you want to reach me, all you have to do is call."

"Thanks." Cally smiled, slipping the card into the pocket of her blazer.

"My father is a great man," Peter said, an uneasy look crossing his face. "But he is also driven. He's been looking for you for a long time, Cally. Hybrids make the best vampire hunters because they can pass among vampires as one of their own. My ancestor was proof of that. My father wants to use you as a weapon against his enemies.

"But now all I know is that I don't want to see you hurt by anyone—and that includes my father." He looked down into her face, his eyes brimming with anguish. "Do you understand that I would betray everything and everyone I've ever known for you?"

Even though she knew it was the worst thing she could possibly do, Cally reached up and cupped Peter's face in her pale hands, pulling his mouth to hers in a deep, sensuous kiss. After a time, with his strong arms embracing her, Peter ground his hips against hers, their breathing growing deeper with each gyration.

As their passion grew, so did Cally's hunger, tormenting her with its raging thirst. She broke free of Peter's questing tongue and pressed her trembling lips against his throat. She could taste the sweat that beaded his skin like mercury and feel the throb of his jugular vein as it pulsed against her fangs. She was tempted to take just the tiniest nip. Just a love bite, really. After all, she probably couldn't turn him into one of the undead even if she wanted to. The real danger lay in her getting carried away and drinking too long and too deep. . . .

"No!" Cally cried out as she abruptly tore herself free of the embrace. "I'm sorry, I can't do this." She quickly gathered up her dropped groceries. "I have to go. I'll call you later."

Peter watched in perplexed silence as Cally effortlessly scaled the wall surrounding the graveyard. As she disappeared over the side to the pavement below, he heard a dry, fluttering sound and saw a moth battering itself against the streetlight outside the gate. He frowned and quickly looked away.

Sheila Monture was snoring lightly in front of the flat screen by the time Cally got home. Cally picked up the half-eaten container of Chinese food and empty bottle of Ancient Age lying on the chaise lounge and tossed them in the kitchen trash. Then she took her grandmother's old afghan blanket out of the front closet and carefully draped it over her mother's sleeping form.

She bent over and placed a kiss on Sheila's upturned cheek, then headed back to the bathroom and turned on the shower.

She stood with her eyes closed under the pulsing jet spray for a half hour, but no matter how hard she tried, she couldn't banish the image of her grandmother smiling into the camera as she stood next to the sworn enemy of the vampire race. Meanwhile Peter's words echoed over and over inside her head:

You don't have to keep living a lie.

CHAPTER 13

"**W**inged flight is our heritage and our destiny."
Coach Knorrig kept her hands clasped behind
her back as she addressed the second-period
aerial exercises class. "But there is more to flying than
flapping your wings and avoiding low-flying aircraft.
Fluttering around in the open sky is one thing; learning
to use echolocation so you can fly in tight, cramped
spaces is something else altogether."

Standing on a high, wide ledge a hundred feet above
the floor of the grotto, Cally was glad that several
girls were between her and Lilith, who was eyeing her
dangerously.

As Coach Knorrig continued her speech on the
importance of close-quarters aerial skills, Cally moved
nearer to the edge for a better view. From here it was
easy to tell that the vast underground chamber had

been made, not created naturally. The stalagmites on the floor far below reminded her of the hedgerows in a garden maze.

Looking down, she was overcome by a burst of vertigo and quickly stepped back. She glanced up and saw the Todd girl staring at her like something she'd scraped off the bottom of her shoe. It would be too ridiculous to plummet headfirst to her death. Then again, Cally wouldn't put it past any of her classmates, especially Lilith, to give her a shove over the ledge when she wasn't looking.

The coach consulted her ever-present clipboard and said, "Maledetto, you're first."

At first Cally thought the twin who stepped forward was Bella, who had been in her shapeshifting class the night before. Then she realized the ribbons the girl was removing from her hair were red, not blue.

"Could you keep these for me?" Bette Maledetto asked timidly, holding the hair ribbons out to Lilith. She was used to having her twin sister's help with such things, but the administration was placing them into separate classes in an attempt to foster independence.

"What do I look like? Your body servant?" Lilith sniffed, eyeing the satin ribbons with distaste.

Seeing a chance to make a much-needed ally, Cally quickly stepped forward. "I'll look after them for you."

"Thanks," Bette said.

Bette walked up to the very edge of the precipice

and lifted her arms high up over her head, her fingers shooting rapidly outward while her thumbs crooked into huge claws. As the bones of her hands warped themselves into a strange new geometry, the skin between her fingers and along her arms expanded and grew into a membranous cape. The tip of her nose pushed upward and back, exposing the nostrils, while her lips peeled back to reveal pearly white fangs. The pointed tips of her ears quadrupled in size while moving to the top of her skull, and her hair was replaced by dark gray fur as soft as moleskin. Her neck retracted, pulling her head in tight between her shoulders, while her chest widened to accommodate a longer reach. The toes of her feet elongated until they were all the same length, the nails curving into ebony talons. Within seconds Bette was leaning forward on transformed legs, the knees of which now bent backward, chittering anxiously to herself as she peered down at the jagged forest of stone below her.

Cally was astounded at how quickly Bette had metamorphosed from a cute, baby-faced teenage girl into a monstrous humanoid bat. The whole transformation, from start to finish, hadn't taken more than a few heartbeats. The thought of having to accomplish the same feat made her own heart drop like a coin down a subway grate.

"Don't be nervous, Maledetto," Coach Knorrig said in a cajoling voice. "You can do it."

Bette contracted her pectoral muscles, bringing her wings down to her sides. Flexing her huge mutated thumbs, she flung herself into the abyss. Her classmates surged forward, jostling one another for the best view as she plunged toward the rocks. Suddenly Bette's arms snapped open as if they were spring-loaded and, cupping her wings against the air rushing past her body, she began to make a vigorous rowing motion. The skin of her wings instantly billowed outward, generating lift that pulled her up and away from the rapidly approaching cave floor.

"Good job, Maledetto! You're doing great!" Coach Knorrig called after her. "Now find a rock and stick to it!"

Bette fluttered over and anchored herself to a stalactite, hanging upside down by her hooked thumbs and clawed feet.

"I hope the rest of you saw what Maledetto did to launch herself," Coach Knorrig said. "Mortimer: I see you've got your hand raised," she said, pointing at Bianca. "What is it?"

"Is this going to be on the test?"

Coach Knorrig sighed and pinched the bridge of her nose with her thumb and forefinger. "There are no written tests for this class, Mortimer. You're graded on physical performance alone."

"Yes, ma'am," Bianca replied sheepishly.

"Okay, now that you lovely ladies have seen how

easy it is to get yourself airborne, I want you lined up single file and in alphabetical order, ready to make your jump."

There was a sudden scurry of bodies and a flurry of voices as the assembled students sorted themselves out by surname. As Cally reluctantly moved to take her place in line, Coach Knorrig caught her by the arm and pulled her aside.

"This doesn't include you, Monture."

"But you said line up. . . ."

"I *know* what I said. And I'm telling you to stand down. If you can't turn into a wolf yet, I'm certainly not going to allow you to make a hundred-foot jump in the hope you *might* grow wings on the way down. Look, kid, can you even wall-crawl yet?"

"Kinda, but not really," Cally admitted, dropping her gaze. Although she was secretly relieved that she wouldn't have to put her flying ability to the test, she was equally embarrassed to be singled out from the others. "But I'm pretty good at jumping. I can take a ten-foot wall."

"Well, that's a start," Coach Knorrig conceded. "But it's a far cry from being able to fly."

"What about my grades? You said this is a performance-based class. What am I supposed to do if I'm not allowed to fly?"

"Run laps."

"But . . ."

"Don't argue with me, Monture," Coach Knorrig said. "If I tell you to run laps, the only thing I want to hear out of your mouth is, 'For how long?' Is that clear?"

"Yes, Coach. For how long?"

"Until I tell you to stop. Now excuse me, I need to get this class going."

With that Coach Knorrig jumped off the ledge and, with a single beat of her wings, joined her remaining students, who were clustered together. With a heavy sigh, Cally headed down the spiral staircase built into the side of the cavern to the floor below.

"Monture!" Coach Knorrig shouted, her voice echoing through the grotto.

Cally slowed her jog down to a walk before finally stopping altogether. She had been running laps so long she'd lost track of time. She looked up and saw Knorrig, still in her winged form, perched atop a nearby stalagmite.

"Hi, Coach," Cally gasped as she bent over to catch her breath, resting her palms on her knees. Although the grotto was a perpetual sixty-three degrees, it was humid. Sweat trickled down her back. "Is class over?"

"I'm sorry, kid. To be honest, I kind of forgot about you. I sent the rest of the girls to the showers a few minutes ago. If you hurry, you should still catch the midnight feeding before your next class."

"Gee, thanks, Coach," she said, fighting the urge to say something snide about how much she appreciated getting a whole ten minutes for mealtime once she finished showering and changing her clothes. Things were craptastic enough already with Coach Knorrig— she didn't need to be running laps backward.

As she headed to the locker room, Cally realized that she still had Bette Maledetto's red hair ribbons in the pocket of her gym suit. She decided to hang on to them. No doubt Bette would eventually come looking for them. Maybe she could use the opportunity to talk to her without Lilith or one of her toadies trying to shut her down.

The locker room appeared to be completely deserted by the time Cally entered. Although she was hacked that she was going to barely have time to eat, at least she had the luxury of changing clothes without being watched. With every other girl in her class wearing La Perla, the fact that she had to buy her panties three to a pack was uniquely humiliating.

As she opened the clean towel hamper, Cally thought she heard a noise coming from the toilet stalls on the other side of the room.

"Hello? Is somebody there?"

She tilted her head to one side, but all she heard was a leaky showerhead dripping. She shrugged and turned back to the hamper; only this time she heard the distinctive sound of a stifled sob.

Cally closed the lid and walked over to the toilets, scanning the floor under the closed stalls. She stopped in front of the last door, under which she could clearly see a pair of legs outfitted in brown penny loafers and white kneesocks.

"Are you okay in there?"

"Go away!" The voice on the other side of the door was so high-pitched it sounded like the owner had just inhaled an entire tank of helium.

"What's wrong with your voice? Are you hurt?"

"No, I'm okay—I mean, no, I'm not hurt. Just go away and leave me alone!" The girl inside the toilet stall began to sniffle and sob quietly to herself again.

"Look, this is silly. Obviously something *must* be wrong or you wouldn't be crying," Cally said, reaching for the stall door handle. "Come out where I can see you."

"No!" the student cried out, her voice climbing so high Cally had to cover her ears with her hands. *"Don't look at me!"*

"Okay! Okay!" Cally said, trying to calm down the other girl. "Is there something I can do to help?"

"I don't think so."

"How can you be so sure of that if you won't even tell me what the problem is?"

"Okay, I'll tell you," the girl on the other side of the stall said after a long pause, "but you have to *promise* you won't tell anyone."

"I promise."

"I'm stuck."

"Stuck?" Cally frowned, unsure of what she meant. "Like on the toilet?"

"No. Like this," the other girl said as she pushed open the toilet stall door.

Cally yelped in surprise before clapping a hand over her mouth. Standing before her, dressed in the uniform of a Bathory Academy student, was a small, slightly built girl with the ears and nose of a giant bat.

"Don't look at me! I'm hideous!" the bat-headed girl squeaked, raising her arms to shield her face.

Cally struggled to regain her composure. "How did this happen?" she asked.

"I'm not exactly sure," the bat-headed girl replied. "I had changed back and was getting dressed when I realized I didn't have my ribbons on me. I tried to remember the last time I saw them, and the next thing I know, I'm starting to change! I ran into the stall the moment I felt it starting to happen. I didn't want any of the other girls to see."

"You're Bette Maledetto?" Cally gasped in amazement.

"Afraid so," Bette squeaked as she nodded.

Cally reached inside her gym suit pocket. "I have your ribbons, if that helps."

"Thanks," Bette said, rubbing the red satin against her furry cheek as if it was a beloved pet. Then she wailed, "What am I gonna *do*? I keep trying and trying to change all the way back, but nothing works!"

"You stay put. I'll get Coach Knorrig."

"No! Don't do that!" Bette pleaded as she grabbed her arm. "She'll report this to the headmistress, I know she will! Everyone here at school already looks down their noses at me and my sister because we're half-bloods! This is the kind of thing they'd love to use as an excuse to prove we don't belong here!"

"That's funny—I thought *I* was the only student here with that problem," Cally said with a bemused smile.

"No, we're legacy students too," Bette squeaked. "Our mama is a Lamia, one of the Old Blood, but our papa is New Blood. Most of the other girls won't have anything to do with us at all, although they don't openly bully us like they do you, for fear of what might happen. The only one who is nice to us is Melinda. The others like to make fun of her because her totem is a panther, not a wolf, like the rest of them. I guess that makes her feel kind of sorry for me and my sister." Something that was probably a look of despair crossed Bette's transformed face. "What's the use? Even if this doesn't end up on my permanent record, I will *never* be able to live it down. Lilith will make sure of it! Her father and our father are old enemies, and she sees to it every chance she gets that we're miserable! I can already hear the others laughing and calling me 'Batty' behind my back." She dropped down onto the toilet seat and began to cry again, daubing at her upturned, leaf-shaped nose with a length of toilet paper still attached to the roll. "I might as well flush my social life down the tubes while I'm in here!"

"Don't get yourself all worked up," Cally said, patting Bette on the shoulder. "That's not going to help anything. Look, you need to decide what's more important: getting a bad grade or being able to walk around without a potato sack over your head. Besides, you can't stay in the girls' locker room for the rest of your life. You've got to come out *some*time. I'll go find Coach Knorrig and explain the situation to her. I'm sure she'll know what to do."

"You're right: there's no other way out of this," Bette said with a sigh, her shoulders dropping in resignation. "It's really nice of you to help me, though. Up until now the only person I've ever been able to count on is my sister."

"Well, the way I see it, we half-bloods need to stick together, right?"

CHAPTER 14

Cally exited the locker room and hurried to Coach Knorrig's office, only to find the door locked. She went back out into the grotto and looked around the stony landscape, hoping to catch sight of the coach. From where she stood, the floor of the grotto resembled a forest full of petrified trees.

"Hello? Coach?"

Cally cocked her head, hoping to catch a response, but all she heard was her own voice echoing through the cavern. As she turned toward Ruthven's side of the grotto, she saw somebody moving between the rock formations.

"Coach! Wait up!" she shouted. Cally hurried toward the figure threading its way through the ground-level labyrinth.

Suddenly a dark figure stepped out from behind a

large rock directly into her path. Cally gave a tiny cry of surprise and fell backward, landing on her butt.

"*Owww!*"

"I'm *dreadfully* sorry! Please, allow me to help you up," the shadowy figure said with a slight, masculine lisp. He extended a hand with fingers nearly twice as long as normal. Cally looked up past the stranger's hand and saw a very tall, gaunt young man dressed in the charcoal slacks, burgundy blazer, and red-and-black tie of a Ruthven's student. The youth's dirty-blond hair was combed back away from his high broad forehead in a pronounced widow's peak, which not only accented his arched eyebrows and pointed ears, but his aquiline nose, large deep-set eyes, and wide, sensual mouth as well. Despite his outré appearance, he exuded a gentility Cally was unaccustomed to in boys her own age.

"I'm sorry if I scared you. I tend to do that." Smiling apologetically, he helped her off the ground.

"I wouldn't say that you scared me—startled is more like it." Cally chuckled as she brushed herself off.

"Yeah, I kinda do that too." He sighed.

"I'm trying to find Coach Knorrig," Cally explained.

"Oh! When I heard someone calling for Coach, I thought they might be trying to find Coach Munn. I'm his student assistant."

"No, I'm looking for Coach Knorrig. Do you know where she is?" Cally asked hopefully.

"She left to run an errand. Last I saw her, she was

headed down the emergency exit," he said, motioning toward the eastern end of the grotto.

"Emergency exit?" Cally frowned.

"The schools came up with the idea for it after the Great Fire. It's a secret tunnel that goes under the East River and comes up at Mill Rock Island, out in the East River's Hell Gate."

"What about this Coach Munn you mentioned—is he still around?" Cally asked hopefully.

"Afraid not," he replied.

"Great!" Cally muttered, rolling her eyes in consternation.

"Perhaps I can be of some help? I *am* a teaching assistant, after all."

"Well, there's this girl in my class . . . turns out she's, uh, kind of stuck."

"Stuck?" he echoed, raising a quizzical eyebrow.

"Yeah—between shapes."

"I *see.*"

"That's the thing, though. She doesn't *want* anyone to see. I was barely able to talk her into letting me go fetch Coach Knorrig."

"Still, I think I can help her out."

"Could you? That would be great!"

"Where is she?"

"She's hiding in the locker room. Come on, I'll show you!"

The smile on his face suddenly disappeared. "The

locker room? You mean the *girls'* locker room?"

"Yeah, where else?"

"It's just that I could get—you know—if anyone saw me go in there . . ." he stammered.

"She's the only one in the locker room. No one else is there. And you said both Coach Knorrig and Coach Munn are gone, so who's left to see you go in?"

"Okay, you've persuaded me," he said with a grin.

"Thanks. My name's Cally, by the way."

"My name's Xander," he replied. "It's my pleasure. And my friends call me Exo."

"Hello? Bette?"

"Who's that?!" Bette squeaked anxiously from her hiding place in the toilet stall.

"Relax, it's just me," Cally replied "Are you decent?"

"*Decent?!?* I look like a bat from the neck up!"

"The reason I'm asking is because I've got a guy with me."

"A *guy*?!?" Bette's voice momentarily disappeared into the ultrasonic register. "I thought you were going to get Coach Knorrig!"

"The coach went out to lunch, I guess. But I found someone who says he might be able to help you," Cally explained.

"Forget it! If I don't want the other girls to see me

like this, I sure don't want a *man* looking at me!"

"Let me talk to her," Xander whispered to Cally. He stepped up to the locked toilet stall, leaning against it so that his mouth was as close to the door as possible. "Hello—Bette, is it? I know you're upset right now and embarrassed," he said, talking in a calm voice as if he was trying to pacify a skittish animal. "But it's nothing to be ashamed of. Getting stuck every now and then is perfectly natural. Believe me, you have nothing to be worried about. You can show yourself to me."

"You *promise* you won't laugh?" Bette asked.

"I promise," he replied solemnly.

"Or scream?"

"Believe me when I tell you it doesn't make *any* difference to me *what* you look like," Xander said with a small laugh.

"I don't know about that," Bette said doubtfully. "I look *really* hideous."

"Would it make you feel any better if I told you I'm an Orlock?"

There was the sound of a bolt being thrown back and the toilet stall door opened just enough for Xander to see a tiny, blood-red eye surrounded by dark gray fur staring back at him.

"The count's son?"

"One of them, anyway," he replied.

"Well, I guess it's okay, then." Bette opened the door

the rest of the way and stepped outside so he could get a better look.

Xander studied her for a long moment, his arms folded so that his left hand cupped his right elbow while he tapped the side of his nose with an overlong index finger.

"Is it bad?" Bette squeaked fearfully, clutching her red ribbons to her chest.

"No, not at all. You just need a little push in the right direction so you can finish the transformation, that's all. There's something called a reversal potion that will solve your problem. Unfortunately, Coach Munn keeps his supply under lock and key. However, I've been studying the formula in my potions class, and I think I can safely replicate it."

"That's great!" Cally said excitedly. "See, Bette? I told you everything would be all right! All Exo has to do is go whip up a batch of reversal potion and bring it back here so you can drink it!"

"Yeahhhh. About that," Xander said uneasily as he rubbed the back of his neck. "The reversal potion actually has a very short half-life and requires a special binding agent in order for it to be bottled and transported. The problem is that the only person who has access to the binding agent is Professor Frid. By the time I make the potion, put it in a vial, and bring it back from the lab at my school, it will be useless. In order for it to work, it must be consumed within a minute or two of being concocted."

"So that means—?"

"We have to smuggle her into Ruthven's."

"*What*—?" Bette's voice made both Cally and Xander wince. "Are you *crazy*? Bathory students caught on the Ruthven campus without a chaperone are automatically expelled! The same goes for Ruthven students coming onto Bathory property! As a matter of fact, if someone walked in on us right now, we'd *all* be tossed out!"

"Would you rather I go and report your condition to Madame Nerezza?" Cally asked.

"No," Bette admitted.

"Then Xander has to smuggle you into the boys' school—and out again."

Bette's mutated upper lip began to quiver and tears welled in her beady red eyes. "I'm *scared*, Cally! I'm not used to doing stuff without Bella."

"If it'll make you feel better, I'll go with you."

"You will? Oh, thank you, Cally!" Bette squeaked, throwing her arms around the other girl's neck. "Thank you! Thank you! Thank you! But aren't you afraid of getting into trouble?"

"The way things are going, I seriously doubt I'm going to be attending Bathory Academy much longer anyway." Cally shrugged. "The way I look at it, what do I have to lose?"

* * *

"Wow, so this is what it's like in the boys' school," Bette whispered in awe as they hurried along the corridor that connected the grotto to Ruthven's School for Boys. Where the corridor leading to the grotto on Bathory Academy's side had been fashioned of natural rock and boasted a barrel-vaulted ceiling, Ruthven's resembled the enclosed walkway of a Gothic monastery.

"We've got to hurry. The grotto and laboratory are normally deserted during mealtime, but there's still a chance we'll be spotted," Xander explained. He pushed the call button for the elevator. "I could try and cast an obscuration spell around the two of you, but that's only of use against being seen by clots."

"What about the elevator operator?" Cally asked. "Aren't you worried about him seeing us?"

"What operator?" Xander asked with a puzzled frown as the doors pinged open, revealing a modern push-button elevator.

Like Bathory, the classrooms for Ruthven's School for Boys were situated underground on three subterranean levels, the third of which was the grotto, which it shared with its sister school. The Gothic architectural look was continued on the second level with an impressive ribbed vault ceiling and pointed arch doorways.

"Here we are," Xander whispered over his shoulder as he opened the door to the potions lab. "Luckily, our master chymist, Professor Frid, is a man of very rigid habits. We have a good fifteen minutes before he returns from lunch."

The floor at the center of the room was covered with strange symbols and half-melted candles, and the walls were lined with stone tables. Xander hurried over to a table in the far corner covered in a jumble of vials, flasks, and tools, including a macabre mortar and pestle fashioned from a human skull and arm bone. He shrugged out of his school blazer and slipped on a stained leather apron. Quickly measuring out liquids and powders from various containers, he poured them into a glass beaker suspended over a small gas flame burner, which he then lit.

"Are you absolutely sure this is going to work?" Bette asked anxiously as she watched him mix black hellebore and powdered mandrake into the madly bubbling mix.

"I'm positive!" he said, giving her a reassuring wink. "We Orlocks have a knack for such things, you know."

Suddenly the lab door opened and slammed shut.

"Someone's here!" Xander whispered, a look of dread on his face. "Quick! Hide!"

Cally nodded her understanding and grabbed Bette by the hand, dragging her along behind her as she ducked under a nearby table.

"Hey—Exo! Is that you?"

Xander turned to see his cousin Jules ambling toward him, a surprised look on his handsome face.

"Yeah, it's me," Xander replied, nervously rubbing his palms against his lab apron.

"What are you doing here?" Jules asked.

"I was about to ask you the same thing."

"I forgot my formula workbook," Jules explained, holding up a battered leather volume bound with metal clasps. "My dad's still holding that trip to Vail over my head if I don't get my grades up. Why are *you* here?"

"Just putting in a little extra-credit work, that's all."

"You're such a spod, Orlock." Jules chuckled.

"Well, it's not like I can get by on my good looks, like some people I know," Xander said with a crooked smile.

"So . . . you wanna come hang after school? Sergei's having a bunch of the guys over. His parents are out in the Hamptons."

"I don't think so," Xander said. "That's not really my scene. Like you said, I'm a spod. Besides, I get the feeling Lilith's uncomfortable with me hanging around."

"I haven't told Lilith about the party yet," Jules said, looking down at his shoes.

"Are you going to?"

"I dunno. Maybe." He shrugged. "It's just that she's been acting so strange lately, you know? Ever since Tanith got, you know, she's done nothing but obsess about that girl at her school, the New Blood."

"Lilith and Tanith were friends, Jules," Xander said pointedly. "She probably misses her. Maybe fixating on the New Blood takes her mind off it."

"Yeah, I guess so," Jules admitted halfheartedly. "I just wish she'd be more like her old self again."

"If that's the case, why don't you try and do something to get her mind off Tanith?" Xander suggested. "Something romantic."

"That's not a bad idea," Jules said as he rubbed his chin. "For someone who's never been on a date, you sure seem to understand women."

"My mom has all these subscriptions to *Cosmo* and stuff like that," Xander said with a laugh. "I read them when my dad's not looking."

"I better be going," Jules said. "Thanks for the suggestion, Cuz! I think it might actually work!"

"Later," Xander called out as his cousin exited the room.

"Who was *that*?" Cally whispered as she climbed out from under the lab table.

"My cousin Jules."

"Your *cousin*?" Cally exclaimed, unable to hide her surprise.

"Couldn't you tell from the family resemblance?" Xander said dryly.

"I didn't mean it like that, Exo."

"That's okay." Xander sighed as he returned to his work on the potion. "I'm used to it. Jules is a babe magnet and I'm a babe *anti*-magnet. I know it, you know it, and the whole world knows it."

"You shouldn't talk that way about yourself," Cally chided, placing her hand on his arm.

Xander paused to flash her a sad smile. "You're a very sweet girl, Cally, but there's no point in deluding myself. The Orlocks might be one of the oldest, richest, and most powerful families in the world—but if there's one thing we're *not*, it's easy on the eyes. Hell, most of us can barely pass for human. I know that I'll never be handsome, and I've come to accept that. I'm comfortable with myself, which is more than a lot of people—vampires included—can say. Now watch out; when I add the final ingredient to the potion, it's gonna fizz like Diet Coke and Mentos."

Xander picked up an unmarked vial and tapped a small measure of powder into the bubbling beaker. The mixture began to foam wildly while changing every color of the spectrum. When it got to lavender, Exo snatched the dripping beaker from the burner, poured out the liquid into a glass, and handed it to Bette.

"Drink it quickly, before it stops bubbling."

Bette sniffed the mixture apprehensively with her upturned bat's nose. "It smells like unwashed gym socks."

"I didn't say it would smell good," Xander replied testily. "I just said it would *work*."

Summoning her courage, Bette closed her eyes and knocked back the contents of the beaker in one gulp. "Ugh! It tastes even nastier than it smells!" she said with a grimace as she wiped the residue from her mouth.

"I didn't say anything about it tasting good, either," Xander reminded her. "How do you feel?"

"Okay, I guess," Bette said as the fur receded from her face and her features returned to their former appearance. "It's kind of weird, though. It's like someone's massaging my face from the inside out."

"I can't believe it!" Cally gasped. "It really worked!"

"Of course it did," Xander said, a hint of pride in his voice. "But you two need to get out of here. The midnight meal will be over any minute now. That means the halls are gonna be full of students and faculty headed back to their classrooms."

"Thank you, Exo," Bette said sincerely. "I won't forget what you did for me. C'mon, Cally—let's go!"

As Cally moved to follow her schoolmate out the door, she suddenly turned back and planted a quick kiss on the side of Xander's cheek. "Thanks for everything, Exo," she whispered in his pointed ear. "You're a great guy, you know that?"

Xander stood there, his mouth hanging open like a fish, one hand cupped over his kissed cheek as if it had just been slapped as he watched Cally hurry out the door and down the hall.

"Orlock, you're such a spod," he groaned.

* * *

Jules de Laval stood in the students' second-floor lavatory, staring down into the sink while he washed his hands. Exo was right about what he needed to do. Then again, Xander had always been the smart one in the family.

If he wanted to get Lilith back to her old self, he needed to keep her mind off the New Blood girl. But how? He remembered what Exo had said about Aunt Juliana's fashion magazines. His own mother had several subscriptions as well, which got him thinking.

Maybe he would place a call between classes and get one of the servants to look through his mother's magazines and find something romantic for him to do. He was deciding to make that his plan of action for the night when he stepped out of the restroom and instantly collided with someone running down the hall.

Jules staggered backward and was about to curse whoever it was for being a clumsy bastard when he realized he was staring not at a fellow Ruthven's student but at a girl.

He stood there in surprise, not simply because Bathory Academy students were forbidden inside Ruthven's, but because the girl standing before him was the New Blood from the park, up close and beautiful.

With her glittering green eyes, moonflower-white skin, and short, strangely cut hair, the girl standing before him was the exact opposite of Lilith and all the other pampered Old Blood girls he had ever known. The red terry-cloth gym suit fit her in all the right places, hugging her boobs and her taut, toned ass, showing off her long, well-shaped legs.

Jules looked past the beauty standing before him and saw, farther down the corridor, Bette Maledetto, dressed in full Bathory uniform. She was leaning out of the elevator, motioning to the New Blood as she kept the doors of the car from closing.

"What in the name of the Founders—?" he managed to sputter.

The girl in the gym suit lifted a finger to her lips. "Please don't say anything!" she pleaded. "If we get in trouble, your cousin does too!"

"How did you get in here? And how do you know who my cousin is?"

"Because Exo smuggled us into the alchemy lab. We were hiding in there when you came to get your homework," she explained.

"I *knew* Exo was up to something!" Jules said. "I just didn't think it involved, you know, *girls*."

Jules looked around to make sure no one else was in the hall before grabbing the girl's hand. His heart began to beat faster as he felt her smooth skin beneath his fingers.

"Tell Bette to follow us," he whispered. "Using the elevator to get back to the grotto is too dangerous now. There's an old stairway on this floor that leads to where you need to go. Not many students know about it, and it's rarely used anymore. It should be safe."

Cally turned and waved for Bette to hurry. Jules led them down a hallway off the main corridor to a small wooden door fitted with a brass handle. The door creaked open easily, revealing a set of tightly winding stairs that led downward into darkness.

"Thank you for helping us." Cally smiled. "I think we can take it from here."

Jules shook his head. "No, it's safer if I go with you," he said. "I can run interference if someone's down there."

As Cally and Bette stepped inside the stairway after him, the door closed behind them on its own. They followed the stairs down, pushing their way through cobwebs. After a few minutes they arrived at another narrow door.

"This opens onto a section of the grotto roughly a couple of hundred yards from the Ruthven's entrance tunnel," Jules explained. "I'll go first to make sure the coast is clear."

He stepped out and looked around for signs of students or faculty but saw none. He reopened the door and signaled for the girls to join him.

"Once again, thank you for your help," the girl in the gym suit said, teasing him with a smile. "It was very gallant of you."

"It was nothing, Miss . . . ?" he said, responding to her flirting tone.

"Cally."

Jules stepped forward and took Cally's hands in his, bowing slightly at the waist as his lips brushed lightly against the curve of her fingers. "*Enchanté*, Cally." Jules smiled.

"The pleasure is mutual, monsieur," she replied, affecting an exaggerated curtsy.

Delighted with their play, Jules and Cally started laughing, but when they heard Bette giggle, Cally blushed. "We better be going," she said, letting go of his hands.

"*Au revoir.*" Jules smiled.

Jules paused to watch the girls dash back to their side of the grotto. He told himself he was only making sure they got back safely, but in reality he just wanted to admire Cally's butt.

CHAPTER 15

W hen Bathory Academy was originally founded,
there was no such thing as a school cafeteria.
But as Victor Todd's blood-banking scheme
grew more and more accepted by the population, that
eventually changed. Now there was a large room set
aside for the students and faculty to take their meals,
filled with tables and chairs straight out of Ikea. At the
back of the cafeteria was a large, triple-door blood bank
refrigerator set into the wall.

As Lilith stepped to the head of the line, she had an
unobstructed view of the racks of stainless steel drawers
stocked with plastic bags full of human blood.

The undead servant in cafeteria whites smiled in
greeting and asked, "What will it be tonight, dearie?"

"I think I still have some of my private stock banked
on reserve," Lilith replied.

"Indeed you do, Miss Todd." The lunch lady opened one of the doors of the refrigerator and reached inside a drawer, withdrawing a blood bag, which she then placed on a plastic cafeteria tray. On the front of the bag was a label marked with a large *AB-* along with the HemoGlobe corporate logo: a single drop of bright red blood superimposed over a world silhouetted in white.

Lilith took her tray and sat down at the nearest available table. Within a minute or two all her friends had joined her. After all, no matter where she sat, it was the popular table.

"Have you seen Annabelle Usher tonight?" Carmen asked as she sat down opposite Lilith, the corner of her mouth pulled into a smirk. She nodded in the direction of a short, pale girl with a round face and dark hair cut in a blunt bob, with what looked like a pair of upside-down *U*s drawn in place of eyebrows. "She's such an utter spod! And look at how dingy her clothes are—doesn't she have more than one skirt and blouse to wear to school?"

Lilith shook her head in disgust. "If a legacy student's family is so hard up they can't provide a dresser for their child, she has no business attending Bathory." She paused and looked around the room. "Speaking of which, where's the newbie?"

"You mean Cally?" Bianca Mortimer asked, missing the point as usual. "I haven't seen her since flight class.

Why? Do you want to talk to her?"

"Did I mention she had the gall to try and lay some pathetic 'why can't we all just get along' speech on me last night? I told her to kiss my ass."

"Lilith's right," Carmen agreed. "We've got enough half-bloods and legacies ruining things for the rest of us here—we don't need a New Blood making things worse."

"I think you're making a mistake," Melinda said suddenly.

The chatter at the table fell abruptly quiet as the other girls turned to stare at Lilith, who was glaring at Melinda like an angry eagle. When she finally spoke, her voice was surprisingly calm.

"What was that?"

"I just think maybe you shouldn't be in such a hurry to make an enemy out of her, that's all," Melinda replied cautiously. "She's not some mousy little spod. You've seen what she can do."

"Are you saying I should be *scared* of her?" Lilith asked, her eyes narrowing into slits.

"No, of course not, Lili," Melinda replied with a nervous laugh.

"I'm not surprised you're taking up for that slut, Melly," Lilith said, venom dripping from every word. "Everyone knows how cozy you are with the Maledetto twins. I guess you want to add the newbie to your collection of lonely girls."

"What are you trying to get at, Lilith?" Melinda growled.

"Oh, come off it, Melly!" Lilith sneered. "Of all the girls at this table, you're the only one who's never had a boyfriend. I wonder why, hmmm? You're too taken by the newbie to see the truth. There's something wrong about her, *seriously* wrong. I knew it from the first moment I saw her! Looking at her sets my fangs on edge."

"You're just jealous," Melinda shot back.

"Jealous?" Lilith barked a humorless laugh. "What's there to be jealous of? She's a weak-blooded loser who can't even shapeshift!"

"She put down the Van Helsing who killed Tanith single-handed," Melinda replied. "That's more than any of us have ever done—including you. I wouldn't call her a weak-blooded loser."

The other girls seated at the table took a collective breath in anticipation of the explosion they knew was sure to follow. Instead Lilith pushed back her chair and, without saying another word, got up from the table and stalked out.

Carmen turned and glowered at Melinda. "Have you gone psycho, talking to her like that?" she snapped. "And for what? To get in the pants of some New Blood skank?"

"You really don't get it, do you?" Melinda asked, shaking her head in disbelief at her friend's utter cluelessness. "If you'll excuse me, I think I'll go and finish having lunch with one of my friends." With that Melinda picked up her tray and moved over to join Bella Maledetto, who was sitting by herself, looking lost and confused without her sister.

Lilith sat on an outcropping fifty feet above the floor of the grotto, her arms wrapped about her legs, her chin resting on her knees as she stared blankly into the darkness that surrounded her. She had to get away from the others, and this was the one place she knew no one would ever think to look for her.

Up to this point in her life, her physical beauty, her father's wealth, and her family's status had provided her with plenty of friends. Indeed, until now she had never had to work at making friends, much less keeping them.

"Friends." That was a laugh. Melinda, Carmen, and the others were like the tiny fish that swim alongside great whites, nibbling at the crumbs that fall from their jaws. Still, it was important to have the right kind of friends if she wanted to remain popular. It wouldn't do to have her pilot fish swimming after another shark.

How would she know she was beautiful, popular, and desirable if she didn't have a circle of fawning friends eager to pay attention to her and tell her how special she was? Without their adulation, admiration, fear, and respect, how could she be sure she even existed at all?

In less than a week, she had lost two friends, all because of Cally Monture. Tanith was dead because of the New Blood's showboating, and now Melinda was openly siding with the whore, defying her in front of the others. She should have bitch-slapped the little traitor until her ears rang. But what good would it have done? The real threat was Cally, not Melinda.

The very thought of the New Blood made Lilith's guts writhe like snakes on a bonfire. It aggravated her that the others didn't sense the *wrongness* in Cally. Although Carmen and a couple of the others were quick to rag on the newbie, Lilith knew it was out of a desire to get on her good side, not because they recognized Cally for what she was: a threat. A threat to *her*, in particular.

There was the sound of voices from the grotto floor below, distracting Lilith from her thoughts. She looked down and saw three figures standing on the Ruthven side of the cavern. One was a male dressed in a Ruthven's uniform while the other two were female, one in a Bathory Academy uniform, the other in a gym suit.

As Lilith watched, the male stepped forward, bowed, and kissed the hands of the girl in the gym suit. With a surge of alarm, Lilith recognized the boy as Jules and the girls as none other than Cally Monture and Bette Maledetto.

❖ 195 ❖

How *dare* she speak to him! Jules was *hers*! Hers and no one else's!

Anger as hot as fresh-poured steel shot through her entire body, spreading like a flood of foul, black, bubbling tar. As she watched the New Blood slut curtsy before her beloved, it was all Lilith could do to keep from swooping down and clawing the filthy little whore's eyes out of her head. Her whole body vibrated with suppressed fury, like a bowstring pulled to its limit, as Cally and Bette ran back across the grotto like a pair of mice sprinting through an open meadow. It would be so easy to shapeshift into her winged form and drive her talons deep into the New Blood's back. As satisfying as the sound of Cally's spine snapping would be, Lilith knew it would pale in comparison to the glory of her screams as she slowly tore the flesh from her body with nothing but tooth and claw.

Lilith looked at her hands and saw they were shaking so badly they seemed in danger of falling off her wrists. Doing her best to control her trembling fingers, she reached inside the pocket of her blazer and removed her tortoiseshell compact.

All she needed was some reassurance, that was all. Just a little something to help her regain control so she could go back to her classmates and smile and pretend that everything was just fine while she plotted out how to get Cally alone so she could kill her.

She popped open the lid, expecting to be rewarded

as before by the sight of her lovely face shining back at her in all its glory. Instead what greeted her was a monster with blood-red eyes and slavering fangs.

Shocked by the sight of her hate-filled face, Lilith threw the offending mirror away. The compact tumbled end over end before finally smashing to pieces on the stones below.

The mirror was destroyed, but the fiend inside it was still very much alive.

CHAPTER 16

The rest of the night Cally was riding high on the adrenaline buzz that came from breaking the rules and getting away with it. As she sat through her remaining classes, she decided that being sent to Bathory Academy wasn't so bad after all.

Granted, the majority of the school's faculty and student body couldn't be counted on to spit on her if she was on fire, but now she could see that not all of them were stuck-up snobs like Carmen and Lilith. Tonight she had made friends with Bette and Exo, and she knew Jules was ready for more. She had to admit that the instructors at Bathory were far better than their counterparts at Varney Hall. Her scrivening instructor, Madame Geraint, was genuinely encouraging and, despite her gruff exterior, Coach Knorrig seemed to be truly interested in helping her realize her potential.

Although she knew she was attending the school under false pretenses, if she was going to survive in the vampires' world, she would need to learn everything she possibly could about Old Blood society, powers, and abilities, just as she'd learned about humanity from her grandmother and about New Bloods at Varney Hall.

She was still feeling optimistic as she left Madame Boucher's history class. School was over for the night, and as she walked to her locker, Cally wondered if she would run into Peter again on her way home. She hoped so, because she really wanted to tell him about everything that had happened at school today.

With Peter she had found someone who understood where she was coming from and didn't judge her for it. Not wanting to leave seeing him to chance, she used the number he'd given her and called him. They quickly arranged to meet in the cemetery after school. Cally's good mood changed, however, as she reached her locker and saw a folded piece of parchment wedged into one of the ventilation slits.

The note, written in the formal chthonic script of the Old Bloods, read: *Someone saw us. She's going to tell the headmistress if we don't give her money. Meet me in the grotto after school, Bette.*

* * *

As Cally stepped out of the elevator into the corridor that led to the grotto, she realized that the gaslights had been extinguished. The darkness was deeper than any she had ever experienced before. It was like she had stepped out of the elevator car and into the deepest ocean trench.

She stood there for a few moments, allowing her eyes to adjust to the complete absence of light. The darkness began to resolve itself into various shades of gray, and she resumed walking down the hall toward the grotto. At the entrance, she heard a fluttering sound from the eastern end of the cave.

"Hello?" she whispered into the pitch blackness. "I got the note."

In answer, she heard a flapping sound. Cally looked up, trying to locate the source of the noise, but all she saw were the hand-carved stalactites that hung from the roof like an inverted forest.

"Where are you?"

"Over here," a voice whispered from the darkness.

As she moved in the direction of the voice, she felt something crunch under her shoes. She looked down and saw that she had stepped on fragments of silvered glass.

Crouching down to pick up a piece of the shattered mirror, she felt a swoosh of wings so close behind her head it raised the hairs on her neck. Cally jumped up and spun around on her heels, her heart racing in her chest, but there was no sign of whatever had just flown past.

"Who's there?" she shouted into the blackness. "Answer me!"

Cruel laughter seemed to come from nowhere and everywhere at once. Cally cursed herself for being fool enough to lower her guard. Even though the school was supposed to be a vendetta-free zone, she still should have known better than to walk right into an ambush.

There was a sudden loud explosion of flapping wings and a furry body with the face of a demon hurtled down from its hiding place, slamming into Cally with the force of a car and knocking her onto her back.

As Cally rolled onto her side, the air shimmered about the batlike creature, and suddenly Lilith was standing over her.

"He's mine! All mine and no one else's, you stupid bitch! Now and forever!" Lilith shrieked, grabbing Cally by the top of her head.

Using a fistful of Cally's hair as a handle, Lilith roughly yanked her to her feet. Cally screamed in pain as she felt her scalp start to tear.

"No one takes what belongs to me and lives to enjoy it!"

"Let go of me, you crazy bitch!" Cally snarled, driving her fist into Lilith's stomach hard enough to make her loosen her grip.

Lilith staggered backward; she stood bowed over, her arms wrapped protectively around her stomach.

Her eyes shone in the darkness as she bit at the air like a rabid animal. "I'm going to kill you, New Blood! I'm going to scatter your guts from here to Broadway!"

"Have you lost your mind?" Cally shouted.

As if in answer, the other girl shrieked and charged headlong at Cally, her fangs bared. Cally nimbly side-stepped her, slamming her elbow into Lilith's back as hard as she could as she zoomed past. Lilith dropped to her knees, staggered by the force of the blow. Cally moved in swiftly, delivering a fierce kick to the ribs.

"I didn't start this, bitch," Cally snarled. "But I'm sure as hell going to finish it!"

Before Cally could deliver another kick, Lilith's body rippled and contorted, to be replaced by that of a snarling wolf. The transformed Lilith whirled about, snapping at Cally with razor-sharp teeth. Cally quickly jumped back, narrowly avoiding the creature's power-ful jaws.

The darkness of the grotto was split by a burst of purple-white light. Lilith yelped in alarm as she cringed at the sight of the strange violet glow shrouding Cally's right hand.

"Get back!" Cally shouted as she held her hand aloft like a torch. Tongues of energy danced on the ends of her fingers like flames on a candelabrum. "I'll fry you if I have to!"

Lilith snarled in defiance and ran on all fours toward the nearest wall. As she reached the rock face, she changed back into human form, scurrying up its craggy surface as quickly as a lizard. Halfway up the wall, she turned her head around on her shoulders 180 degrees to spit at her adversary below.

"Do you realize what Madame Nerezza will do to you when she finds out about this?" Cally shouted up at her.

"Like I'm worried about what that dried-up cow will do!" Lilith retorted. "I'm a blood relative of the founder of this school and my family is its biggest sponsor! I can do whatever I want at Bathory! And I want you dead, New Blood!"

Lilith's features melted and shifted yet again, becoming those of a monster bat. She pushed herself off the wall, spreading her wings to their full span. Cally ducked as Lilith rushed toward her, but not before her attacker raked her back with a razor-sharp talon. Cally put a hand to her shoulder and it came back wet and red.

"First blood is mine yet again!" Lilith crowed in a high-pitched voice. "Face it, newbie: you're no match against me!"

Cally ducked behind one of the stalagmites as Lilith swooped down low again, her grasping talons extended like landing gear. Cally raised her hand and an arc of lightning shot from her palm. With an angry ultrasonic shriek, Lilith flew back up into the air, disappearing to the upper reaches of the grotto. Cally scanned the cathedral-like ceiling, trying desperately to figure out where her attacker had gone, but Lilith was too well hidden among the shadows.

Cally was in real trouble, and both of them knew it. Although she and Lilith were equally matched when it came to hand-to-hand combat, she couldn't compete against Lilith's ability to shapeshift or fly. In fact, the only real weapon she had in her arsenal was her stormgathering, and since she'd missed her first shot, it was going to take time and concentration to gather another charge. Cally prayed that Lilith didn't know that and would continue to keep her distance. Her only hope of surviving was getting out of the grotto and over to the elevator. She probably wouldn't make it to the door without Lilith's claws buried in her spine, but she had to take the chance.

Calling up all her courage, Cally dashed as fast as she could through the labyrinth of stalagmites and columns. All of a sudden, from the depths of the cave came an awful shriek, like that of a damned soul put to the flame. Cally looked over her shoulder and saw Lilith plummeting toward her with talons extended, eyes burning with baleful glee, like an ancient harpy snatching up a hapless victim.

Realizing she was as good as dead if Lilith pinned her to the floor from behind, Cally turned and jumped as high as she could, meeting her adversary in midair. Throwing out her arms in a grotesque parody of an embrace, she pinned Lilith's wings and together they plummeted to the ground.

Unable to gather the lightning needed to defend herself, Cally desperately tried to force Lilith's head back as they rolled around on the hard rock floor of the grotto. Sensing her adversary's weakness, Lilith lunged forward and sank her teeth deep into Cally's right shoulder. Cally screamed in agony as Lilith shook her like a terrier would a rat.

Without warning, Lilith abruptly surrendered her death grip on her enemy. Even through a pain-filled fog, Cally could clearly see shock and surprise in Lilith's beady little bat eyes.

Cally didn't know why Lilith had faltered in her attack, but she wasn't going to question her good luck. Summoning her remaining energy, she used the slight opening to hurl a bolt of electricity from her hand, sending Lilith flying backward. Cally got to her feet and went to where her opponent lay on the floor, whimpering in pain as tendrils of smoke rose from her scorched pelt.

As she stood over her, Lilith raised her head and glared defiantly up at Cally. "Go ahead! What are you waiting for—?" she spat as fur melted away to be replaced by blond hair and perfect tanned skin. "Kill me and get it over with!"

Cally looked down at her clenched right hand, which still glowed with electric fire, then back at Lilith. She took a deep breath and closed her eyes. The crackling nimbus flickered and faded away to nothing.

"No, Lilith," Cally said. "Believe it or not, I don't want to kill you."

"That's bullshit!" Lilith growled. "Stop toying with me and just do it!"

"Will you knock it off with the 'please kill me' routine? I'm trying to be nice here, although I really don't know *why* I should bother."

"Don't pretend you don't know why I did this, you slut!" Lilith snarled. "I warned you what would happen if you didn't stay away from what is mine! I saw you with Jules earlier! You're trying to steal him from me, aren't you? Just like you're stealing my friends! That's why you've followed me to the school, isn't it? To rob me of what's mine!"

"Whoa! Will you just calm down for a minute?" Cally said, holding up her hands for silence. "Look, Lilith—I realize what you saw must have looked bad, but there's an innocent explanation behind it. I'm not interested in your boyfriend, and he's not interested in me—"

"I never said he was!" Lilith snapped.

"Whatever the case, you have absolutely nothing to worry about in that department. If you don't believe me, you can ask Jules himself. He'll tell you the truth. You *do* trust him to do that, don't you?"

"Of course! Jules is my promised. He would never lie to me."

"I'm glad to hear it. As for the reason I'm here at Bathory—you've got it all wrong. Despite what you might think, I haven't been stalking you. I'm not looking to usurp your life. I'm only going to school here because my father threatened to stop sending money to my family if I didn't."

"Your father?" Lilith's eyes narrowed to slits.

"Don't ask me why it's so important to him." Cally sighed. "I've never met the guy. I don't even know his name. Look, I realize we're probably never going to be friends, but there's no need to kill each other over a stupid misunderstanding."

Lilith stared silently at the ground for a moment and then looked back up at Cally. "Are you going to tell the headmistress about what happened here?"

"I won't mention it if you don't bring up seeing me sneak out of the boys' school."

"Agreed, then." Lilith nodded.

"Here, let me help you."

"Don't touch me!" Lilith snarled, slapping aside Cally's hand as she got to her feet. "I *still* don't like you, New Blood, and I *certainly* don't trust you! And what I said before still goes: stay away from me and keep away from my friends! And if I *ever* see you talking to Jules again, I'll finish tearing you to pieces!"

With that, Lilith's arms unfurled into wings and she shot into the darkness. Cally stood and watched to make sure she was really gone, just to be on the safe side, before heading back to the elevator.

She hoped her mother would be asleep by the time she got home. Even though her wounds had already healed, she knew Sheila would definitely freak out if she saw the blood on her blazer and blouse. The last thing she needed was her father learning she'd gotten into a fight at school. And with the daughter of Victor Todd, no less.

CHAPTER 17

Leaving Bathory Academy, Cally was relieved to find the streets empty. After her confrontation in the grotto, she didn't want anyone to know that she relied on the subway for transportation. The last thing she needed was Lilith waiting to jump her as she headed for the number six.

As she walked toward the Eighty-sixth Street station, Cally couldn't wait to be back in Williamsburg, feeling the warmth of Peter's embrace. She was full of stories to tell him except, she suddenly realized, she'd better leave out the part about Jules kissing her hands— and her fantasizing about how it would have felt if he had kissed her on the mouth instead. As much as she would enjoy sharing the details of her life with Peter, a girl still needed to keep a few secrets.

She was lost in thought when a sleek black limousine

pulled up alongside her. Cally rolled her eyes in disgust. Just what she needed to make her night complete: getting cruised by some rich perv on the prowl.

There was a throaty, electric purr as the heavily tinted passenger window slid down, revealing a middle-aged man with graying temples wearing wraparound sunglasses and dressed in an Armani suit. Cally caught the smell of fine Cuban cigars and top-shelf bourbon radiating from him like expensive cologne.

"Would you like a ride, Miss Monture?" the older man asked.

"Get lost, buddy," she replied flatly before coming to a halt and blinking in surprise. "Hey, wait a minute!" she said, turning back to stare at the man in the sunglasses. "How do you know my name?"

In answer to her question, Bella and Bette Maledetto leaned forward.

"Hi, Cally!"

"Hello, Cally!"

"Oh! I'm sorry! I didn't realize you were Bella and Bette's father!"

"That's quite all right, my dear." Mr. Maledetto chuckled. "The offer still stands nonetheless."

"I appreciate it, sir," Cally said. "But I was just on my way to catch the subway. . . ."

"The train?" Mr. Maledetto snorted in distaste. "A lovely young girl such as you taking the subway at this time of the morning? I would *hate* to think what might happen!" The passenger door of the limo suddenly swung wide, as if opened by a phantom hand. "Please, allow me to drive you home," he said, gesturing for her to enter the car. "I *insist*."

Cally climbed into the limo, making herself comfortable on the seat facing opposite her host and his daughters.

"Bette told Papa what you did for her at school," Bella said.

"Indeed you did, my pet," her father said, reaching over to pat Bette's hand. "Miss Monture, I was hoping you would allow me to repay your kindness. What you did for my Bette speaks of a true depth of character. You can't find that kind of substance among the young anymore—at least not in this country."

"Thank you, Mr. Maledetto."

"Please, call me Vinnie!" he said with a smile.

"Not *the* Vinnie Maledetto?" Cally gasped in surprise. Suddenly what Bette had said earlier about the other girls at the school being scared of her and her sister made a lot more sense. Their father was the undisputed leader of the Strega, one of the oldest and most successful criminal secret societies in the history of the world.

"Afraid so." He chuckled. "We Maledettos value our friends, especially those who understand honor and loyalty. So as of tomorrow, I'll be sending one of my drivers to your home to take you to and from school for the rest of the year."

"You don't have to do that, Mr. Maledetto!" Cally protested.

"It's the *least* I can do!" he said, dismissing her objection with a wave of his hand. "The truth of the matter is, even if you had not come to my daughter's aid this evening, I still would have sought you out, my dear. You see, I have heard some *very* interesting things about you from a mutual acquaintance."

Cally frowned. "Who might that be?"

"Coach Knorrig."

"Coach talked to you about me?" Cally asked, even more puzzled than before.

"Yes, she did. In fact, she came to see me earlier this evening. You see, she and I have something of an arrangement. She keeps me abreast of which students of hers possess potential. One of your talents is storm-gathering, is it not?"

"Yes, sir."

"Stormgathering is a rare ability. Most vampires nowadays can't muster up more than a fog. One of the last who could gather lightning was Morella Karnstein herself. Did you know that?"

Cally flashed back to the portrait of the woman with the haunting eyes and red hair, the one Lilith claimed to be descended from. "No, sir," she admitted.

"The reason I am telling you this is because Victor Todd has long been a thorn in my side. It would seem his daughter holds a similar dislike for you," Maledetto said, pointing to the blood drying on her clothes.

"How do you know she was the one who attacked me?" Cally asked in amazement.

"I can smell her on you," Maledetto explained. "When you have lived as long as I have, child, you come to know the scent of your enemy's blood."

Cally was about to say that he must be mistaken, since she wasn't the one who had drawn blood in the battle, then thought better of it. Something told her Vinnie Maledetto wasn't the kind of man you contradicted.

"But before we go any further, I want to make one thing perfectly clear." Maledetto leaned forward so that his face was inches from her own. He pushed his sunglasses down the bridge of his nose, revealing eyes as black as olives. "Whether New or Old, blood is blood, am I right?"

"Yes, sir," she replied quietly.

"I like you, Cally," Vinnie Maledetto said as he leaned back in his seat and removed a Havana from the humidor built into the limo's armrest. "Something tells me that with the proper friends, you will go *very* far in this world of ours. Especially if those friends are the enemies of your enemy's father."

Jules had just checked his watch when the door buzzer finally announced Lilith's arrival. He was surprised to see that she was still dressed in her Bathory Academy uniform. Normally Lilith couldn't get out of it fast enough.

"Where were you?" he asked. "I was starting to get worried."

"Something unexpected came up," she explained. "I had to stay after school for a little bit."

"Did you get it taken care of?"

"Not really," she replied, shaking her head. "So why did you want to meet me over here? I thought we were going out tonight."

"Yeah, well, my folks are away, and since I have the place to myself, I thought maybe it would be nice if we stayed in tonight. We haven't done that in a long time."

"Yeah, you're right; that would be nice," she agreed quietly.

"Lili, are you okay?" he asked worriedly. "You seem real distracted."

"I just have a lot on my mind right now."

"Are you still upset about Tanith?"

"No, not anymore," she admitted.

"I'm glad to hear it." He sighed in relief.

Lilith looked up into his face, as if searching for some sign only she could see. "Jules—I saw you with Cally and Bette in the grotto tonight."

"What?" Although he felt sharply annoyed, he tried to keep it from showing in his voice. "You saw us?"

"Jules, how *could* you? You kissed her hand!" Lilith wailed, her eyes starting to tear. "You *know* how much I hate that girl!"

Jules kept his face as unreadable as a mask as he cast about for a way out of the situation he now found himself in. At least she wasn't yelling at him. Lilith was virtually impossible to deal with when she was mad. When she was weepy and emotional, that meant she was feeling inadequate, which meant he could work her insecurity to his advantage by making her doubt herself.

"Lilith, I was just helping out Exo. I realize Vinnie Maledetto and your father have bad blood between them, but I'm not stupid enough to offend one of his daughters. Besides, I didn't kiss Bette Maledetto's hand or any other part of her!"

"No, not her!" Lilith snapped. "The New Blood!"

"What do you mean?" Jules said, pretending he didn't know what she was talking about.

"You mean you didn't *recognize* her?" Lilith asked, eyeing him suspiciously.

"I didn't get that good a look at her in the park," he replied. "I was too preoccupied with the Van Helsings."

"You like her, don't you? I saw you looking at her when you thought no one was watching," Lilith said accusingly.

Jules laughed and shook his head. "Lili, you have

absolutely nothing to be jealous about! I was just being polite, that's all. The only reason I was with her in the first place was as a favor to Exo. There's nothing more to it than that."

"So, you're not attracted to her at all?" Lilith asked, her tone more hopeful than before.

"Of course not!" he lied. "Besides, I think Exo's kinda sweet on her."

"Exo and Cally?" Lilith couldn't help but giggle at the idea of the two of them together.

Jules brushed a stray strand of hair out of Lilith's face as he kissed her on the forehead. "You and your overactive imagination! You're always finding things to worry about that aren't really there. That's why I thought it would be nice to take your mind off things tonight."

"How so?" she asked.

"You'll see," he said with a mischievous smile. "But you have to trust me first. Do you? Do you trust me, Lili?"

Lilith looked into his eyes and smiled. "Of course I do."

Reaching inside his pocket, Jules pulled out one of his father's black silk handkerchiefs. "Turn around so I can blindfold you."

"How do I know you won't simply tie me up and ravish me?"

"Like I said, you have to trust me."

"Don't get me wrong," she said as he knotted the handkerchief over her eyes. "I have no problems with being ravished!"

"That's my Lili." He chuckled. "Now give me your hand."

"What are you doing?" She giggled nervously as Jules took her hand, leading her from the formal living room in the direction of the stairs.

"It's a surprise."

"What kind of surprise?"

"If I told you that, then it wouldn't be a surprise anymore, would it?" He laughed. "Oops. Watch out. Here comes a step. And another."

"Jules, this is crazy!" She reached up and fumbled with the knot on the blindfold. "I'm taking this thing off!"

"Don't you dare!" he said, pulling her hands back down. "I know you like to be in control of whatever situation you're in, just like your dad, but you've got to learn to just relax, Lilith."

"That's a sure way of getting me horny." She laughed. "Compare me to my father!"

"Would you rather I compared you to your mom?"

"Point taken."

A flight of stairs and several tangled embraces later, they reached the second floor.

"Can I take this thing off yet?" she asked.

"Just one more second." There was a sound of

curtains being pulled back, followed by a glass door being pushed along its track. "Okay, you can look now."

Jules removed the blindfold from her eyes, smiling expectantly. Lilith looked past him onto the large balcony and saw dozens upon dozens of lit candles arranged about the terrace.

"It's beautiful!" she gasped.

"Come outside," he said, gesturing for her to follow him. "I have another surprise."

Lilith stepped out onto the candlelit patio. With a flourish, Jules handed her a small, dark blue box from De Beers.

"Open it, Lili," he urged, eager to see her reaction and reap his reward.

Lilith untied the red ribbon and opened the box slowly. She was thrilled to find a slender white gold chain attached to a heart-shaped pendant encrusted with black and white diamonds.

"Oh, Jules! It's gorgeous!" she exclaimed.

"Do you like it?"

"Like it? I love it! Here, help me put it on!" She pulled her silky blond hair up and turned around so he could fasten the chain around her neck. Once the latch was secure, she quickly turned back, peering anxiously into his cat-green eyes. "How do I look?"

"You look beautiful." He smiled, gently caressing

her cheek with the back of his hand.

Jules was congratulating himself on pulling it off when Lilith's smile suddenly flickered and disappeared, like a flame caught in a strong draft. "I know this sounds weird, but if our families had never promised us to each other, would you have picked me on your own?"

"Of course," he replied with all the conviction he could muster.

"What if your father told you that the marriage contract had been changed? That you were to be promised to someone else? Would you do as you were told or would you stay with me, even if it meant surrendering your bloodright?"

"That's wild," Jules said with a laugh. "What's the point in worrying about something that couldn't possibly happen in the first place? Why not ask me if we'd still be together if I looked like Exo and you weighed three hundred pounds?"

"Yeah, I guess you're right," she said. "You know, Tanith once told me I was lucky that I was promised to you. I thought she just meant you were good-looking. But now I realize it was more than just that."

Jules took her hands in his and brought them to his lips, kissing them as he had Cally's. "I've got some AB neg laced with bourbon warming in the kitchen."

"Yum. My favorite."

"I aim to please." He smiled as he headed back into

the penthouse. "Why don't you just enjoy the view while I go get us something to drink? I'll be back in a couple of minutes."

Lilith walked to the edge of the terrace and looked out at the concrete spires and canyons of the city. The wind from the river played with her hair, gently spinning it around her head like a spiderweb made of gold. She glanced down at the sparkling diamond pendant resting against her breastbone and wrapped her fingers about it possessively.

When Lilith had first crossed the New Blood's path, she had felt a deep and instant hatred. Most of the time when Lilith didn't like someone, it was because they were boring or weren't willing to do what she wanted. But the animosity she felt toward Cally was fueled by something far more primal: threat.

At first she couldn't understand why she should feel so intimidated by a mere New Blood, stormgatherer or not. After their fight in the grotto, she knew the answer to that question, and it did nothing to assuage the fears that had been haunting her.

Like all vampires, she could identify the blood of a kinsman by taste, even if it was no more than a pinprick. The moment Cally's blood filled her mouth, Lilith was so shocked she dropped her guard, allowing her foe to get the upper hand. She had fully expected Cally to kill her then and there. But when she'd spared her life, Lilith realized that the other girl had no clue about what was going on.

One of her father's favorite sayings was the one about knowledge being power. Now, after all these years, she was finally coming to appreciate what that meant. She had no intention of telling Cally the truth, and she wasn't going to let her father find out that she knew. She would use his secrets against him, just as he had planned to use them against her. She would have to be far more careful in the future, though—she didn't want to tip her hand by attacking again until she had figured out her father's agenda.

Looking out at the twinkling lights of the city, Lilith felt her own power surging. When the time came to act, she would do so—without mercy.

The marriage contract that Victor Todd had taken out with Jules's family was a simple one. All that was required was for a son of the de Lavals to marry a daughter of the Todds. And since there was only one son and one daughter, there had never been any doubt about what their destiny would be.

But now, where once there was one Todd daughter, suddenly there were two.

Ever since she was a little girl, Lilith had dreamed of the day when she would finally become the awesome real-life princess she always deserved to be. Being super-rich was one thing, but being an actual member of the Old Blood aristocracy was a totally different kind of power. Once she and Jules were married, her control of everyone and everything in New York City would be complete and unchallenged. After all these years, there was no way she was going to allow her storybook ending to be ruined.

She heard Jules's footsteps coming closer as he returned with their drinks, and she tossed her fine hair defiantly. She was going to live happily ever after, damn them all; nobody had better get in her way—including Prince Charming!

GLOSSARY

BEREFT: Vampires who have had their bloodrights usurped are bereft. They have the choice of agreeing to serve as vassals to the usurper of their bloodright in exchange for protection, opting to start fresh as New Bloods, or becoming an instructor at one of the private schools.

BLOODRIGHT: The ability to control all the undead created by a particular bloodline is the bloodright. When the head of a vampire family dies, he or she passes along this bloodright to the appointed heir. To inherit, the heir must drain the blood of the dying patriarch or matriarch just before death, reducing the body to dust. Some bloodrights date back as far as ancient Sumer. This is how a vampire who might be only a hundred years old (or even younger) can end up controlling vast legions of undead. The heir also gains command of all the humans under his or her parent's mental control. However, should vampires battle each other in hand-to-hand combat, the loser's bloodright can be taken or usurped. A bloodright also includes an increase in certain powers.

BOUND: Being bound is the equivalent of being married in human society. Vampire couples are bound relatively young, although their peak childbearing years are between 100 and 350. Childbirth is still a dangerous proposition for female vampires, and many of them still die in labor. Multiple births are rare, and few can produce more than two children in a lifetime. Of course, most male vampires remarry and reproduce more children after the death of a spouse. Old Blood marriages are arranged between the heads of the families as a means of consolidating power.

CELLAR: Living, captive donors are harvested in the cellar. Slang for a private blood bank.

CHTHONIC SCRIPT: The written language the original Founders of the vampire race brought with them from their home dimension is known as chthonic script. It is the written language of Hell.

CLOTS: If you want a derogatory term for humans, call them clots.

DEMI-SIBLINGS: Vampires who share one parent in common are demi-siblings. Given the high infant mortality rate and incidences of death during childbirth, it is common for vampire males to have a number of brides during their lifespan. Demi-siblings decades apart in age are common.

DONOR: A captive human who is used to produce blood on a daily basis, utilizing modern blood-banking technology, not unlike a milk cow.

EMPTIES: Depleted donors are empties.

FLEDGLING: A young vampire who has yet to fully mature. A vampire is a fledgling from birth until he or she is capable of creating undead, roughly anywhere from twenty-one to twenty-five years of age.

THE FOUNDERS: Venerated by their descendants as demi-gods in a form of ancestor worship, these are the original thirteen founders of the modern vampire race. The Founders were batlike demons born of Hell who were summoned to this dimension by a wizard over twenty thousand years ago. When the wizard died unexpectedly, they found themselves stranded on this mortal plane. At first numbering a hundred, the "brothers" soon warred among themselves to decide who would become king of their new home. When only thirteen were left, they declared a truce and scattered to various corners of the globe so as not to compete with one another. Eventually they became the progenitors of the entire vampire race.

HALF-BLOOD: A true-born vampire who is of mixed-caste parentage, having one parent who is Old Blood and one who is New Blood.

HYBRID: The product of a human-vampire mating is a hybrid. Hybrids are distrusted by true-born vampires, as they are often used as living weapons by professional witch finders and vampire hunters, the most infamous example being the hated Pieter Van Helsing.

LACED BLOOD: Blood that has been taken from humans kept on a continuous feed of alcohol or drugs.

MINION: A weaker, less powerful vampire who attaches him- or herself to a more-powerful vampire in hopes of protection. Unlike vassals, minions have not been usurped and have willingly chosen to serve their liege lord.

NEG: Slang for *negative blood type*.

NEWBIE: Old Blood slang for *New Blood*.

NEW BLOODS: Those true-borns descended from vampires who have had their ancestral bloodrights usurped by outsiders and have chosen to try to rebuild their legacy from the ground up. Although they might have comparatively weak powers, New Bloods aren't necessarily poor; indeed, some are extremely wealthy. They simply don't have the millennia of passed-along genetic/blood-based power and bloodright that the Old Bloods enjoy.

OLD BLOODS: Those true-borns with long, unbroken bloodrights, some of which extend all the way back to original demon ancestors. Old Bloods command vast legions of undead servants and have powers that can include stormgathering, beast mastery, shapeshifting, and mind control as well as innate magical abilities that enable them to cast spells and make potions.

OLDIE: New Blood slang for *Old Blood*.

POZ: Slang for *positive blood type*.

PRIVATE STOCK: Blood "made to order" to suit the tastes of a particular client.

PROMISED: The equivalent of being betrothed in true-born vampire society. Vampire children are promised to each other by their elders, who usually draw up a bondage contract that lists how many children and of what gender shall marry between the families. However, New Blood families often break from this tradition, allowing their children to secure "love matches."

RED: Slang for *blood*.

SCRIVENER'S TALON: A piece of wood or, in some cases, stone carved to resemble a crooked talon. It is the traditional writing instrument of the vampire race and is designed to resemble the claw of their ancestors.

SCRIVENERY: An underground bunker that is a cross between an archive and a library, where the legal documents, diaries, genealogies, and other writings of the vampire race are stored beyond the reach of humans. It also means a place where scriveners are employed making copies of pertinent documents by hand.

SLUMMING: The act of going to areas where the dregs of human society can be found with the intent of either feeding or amusing oneself by terrorizing them.

SPOD: Someone who is extremely studious; a nerd or a geek.

STAKED: Slang for being killed by vampire hunters.

STORMGATHERER: A true-born capable of gathering lightning, blizzards, tornadoes, and the like. While all vampires have this ability to some degree, it is rare to find one capable of gathering more than a heavy fog or drizzling rain.

STREGA: A supernatural criminal society that has its origins in ancient Rome and Greece. Although founded and run by vampires, the Strega employs witches, werewolves, and other assorted supernatural creatures as well. It is rumored that the Strega will sell their services to any and all willing to pay the price—including humans.

SYNOD: The governing body that oversees the laws and rituals of the true-born vampire race. The Synod is overseen by the Lord Chancellor, who serves as the final judge when it comes to deciding disputes between various families. The Lord Chancellor is also responsible for meting out punishment for those accused of breaking the laws of vampire society. The most grievous transgressions are those that expose its existence to the world at large, whether by aggression, accident, or neglect.

TAP: Slang for drinking blood straight from the vein.

THRALL: A living human who is under the mental control of a vampire. Not all thralls are aware of their condition. Thralls can run the gamut from common servants needed to work during the daylight hours to such people as politicians, heads of state, clergymen, and leaders of finance.

TOTEM FORM: The animal shape a vampire takes when he or she shapeshifts. While the wolf is the most common, not all vampires share this totem. Depending on their ancestry, some turn into big cats, such as panthers, lions, and tigers, while others take the form of serpents, such as pythons, cobras, and anacondas.

TOTENTANZ: The vampire equivalent of a funeral, although in practice it bears a closer resemblance to an Irish wake. Following the death of a vampire, friends and family gather for a ritual party that consists of feasting, dancing, and general roistering, basically defying death's hold. Mourning and tears are forbidden. The longer the party, the greater the tribute to the deceased. In ancient times, a totentanz could go on for weeks, if not months.

TRUE-BORN: Vampires distinguish themselves from the undead by calling themselves true-born. True-born are those who are born of vampire parents. It refers to both Old Blood and New Blood. True-borns are essentially living vampires. Although practically immune to all human diseases and capable of regenerating everything but a head or a heart, true-borns are not immortal. They can live up to eight hundred years, provided they are not killed by vampire hunters or, more likely, a rival vampire. During the first twenty-five years of their lives they age identically to humans, but when they finally mature into "adulthood," their aging slows to one tenth of a human's. The last milestones that mark a true-born's maturation are first their inability to be photographed, followed by losing their reflections, and finally gaining the ability to produce undead with their bites. Infant mortality is still very high among the true-born, and every pregnancy is risky for the mother. Advances in fertility medicine are a recent development but one that might not work as well for them as hoped.

TRUE TONGUE: The ultrasonic language first spoken by the Founders.

UNDEAD: Humans killed by a vampire's bite come back to life as the undead. Although they have been altered into something no longer human, neither are they vampires.

Unlike their masters, the undead cannot shapeshift, nor can they fly. Most importantly, they cannot replicate themselves through biting humans. However, they are immortal, though they will spontaneously combust when exposed to direct sunlight. The undead are important to the vampires' daily existence because they do the scut work the true-born are loathe to do—laundry, shopping for essentials, household care, child care, gardening, bookkeeping, security, etc. They are utterly loyal to their masters because, like a queen bee and her beehive, should the vampire controlling them be killed by a vampire hunter, they die as well. Vampire families that have acquired numerous undead over the centuries have learned to warehouse their surplus, placing them in a form of suspended animation until they are needed. A vampire who is extremely wealthy but has few undead servants is socially inferior to one who might be considerably poorer but has numerous undead. Vampires take particular care in the management of their undead, and those who are viewed as being negligent in providing for their legions are dealt with harshly.

USURP: To take another vampire's bloodright by force. This occurs during hand-to-hand combat between rival vampires, when the stronger of the two drinks his or her opponent dry or tears his or her heart out of the chest and devours it.

USURPER: A vampire who has taken a bloodright he or she has no recognized right to. Although a usurper can be from within the same family, such as a younger sibling or cousin, more often than not they are not directly related to the victim.

VAN HELSINGS: The slang term for vampire hunters and those who work for the Van Helsing Institute (VHI) in particular.

VASSAL: A vampire whose bloodrights were usurped and has sworn fealty to his or her usurper in exchange for protection and the possibility of being allowed to later remarry into the stolen bloodline.

VENDETTA: A running blood feud between either individuals or whole families. Vendettas are most often pursued by envious rivals, bereft vampires looking to reclaim stolen bloodrights, jilted lovers, or wronged friends.

VENDETTA-FREE ZONE: Designated areas where vendettas cannot be pursued are vendetta-free zones. One such universal vendetta-free zone is the school system. The various schools where vampires send their young to be educated are off-limits. Pupils are considered off-limits too. They cannot be poached and are immune from long-standing family rivalries. Once they graduate—or drop out—the gloves come off. Any illegal attacks on school-age fledglings by adult vampires are cause for extreme measures by the Synod, the governing body that enforces the laws of the vampire race.

WEAK-BLOODED: Vampires deemed inferior and/or otherwise unsuited to assume the family bloodright are weak-blooded. When there is more than one child, the head of the family must choose which offspring is most fit to inherit. Parents place a high value on aggression as well as physical strength and stamina, followed by various supernatural abilities. Whichever child is deemed the strongest—and therefore most capable of defending the bloodright from usurpers—is appointed heir, while all others are deemed weak bloods. Weak-blooded siblings or demi-siblings must spend the rest of their lives supporting the chosen heir. They are forbidden to marry or reproduce (at least with other vampires). And when their time comes, they must surrender their blood—and whatever undead and personal wealth they've accumulated over the centuries—to either their strong-blooded sibling or their sibling's heirs. The only variations occur when an anointed heir is destroyed before a bloodright can be passed along or when families wish to cement relations by marrying their weak-blooded children to another family's strong-blooded heirs.

LILITH AND CALLY

SHARPEN THEIR CLAWS IN

NIGHTLIFE

A VAMPS NOVEL

CHAPTER 1

With its airy, open spaces, Bergdorf Goodman evoked a sense of uncluttered gentility that was a world away from the funky boutiques and consignment stores Cally Monture normally shopped. Indeed, it felt more like a museum, except that she was surrounded by mannequins in slinky evening clothes.

Cally browsed the racks with her new friends, Bella and Bette Maledetto, in search of gowns suitable for the upcoming Rauhnacht Grand Ball—all the while taking mental notes on the textures, lines, forms, and colors used by the high-end labels. With a little luck, she hoped to be able to replicate some of them on her sewing machine back home.

"*Ooh!* What about *this* one?" Cally asked, holding up a sleeveless Dolce & Gabbana black matte jersey gown with a gathered bust and plunging V-line.

"It's very nice, but don't you think it's a little too revealing?" Bella frowned.

"Duh!" Melinda Mauvais said. A tall, attractive sixteen-year-old with smooth, mocha-colored skin and smoldering jade-green eyes, she was easily the most exotic of the quartet. "The whole point of the Grand Ball is advertising you're eligible!"

"It's just not my style," Bella insisted.

Cally rolled her eyes, unsurprised by her friend's reply. Bella's fashion sense was nonexistent, and her sister's wasn't any better, given that they dressed exactly alike. Not that the whole Tokyopop look didn't work every now and then, but only if you were trying to be *ironic*. The only way anyone could tell them apart was by the color of the ribbons in their hair: blue for Bella, red for Bette. Luckily, the twins were aware they needed all the help they could get, which was why Cally and Melinda had been asked to accompany them.

Cally decided to try her luck with the other twin. "What do you think, Bette?"

"I think it's sexy," Bette said. Since she was ten minutes older than her twin, Bette liked to think she was the more mature.

"You need to pick something out, Bella. After all, the Grand Ball is next weekend!" Melinda reminded her.

"What about you? Do you have something picked out for the Grand Ball, Melly?" Cally asked.

"As a matter of fact, my personal shopper called to tell me the alterations to my Valentino are finished. You want to go with me?"

"What about us?" Bella and Bette asked in unison.

"Why don't you go take another look at those Vera Wangs over there?" Cally suggested as Melinda dragged her off in the direction of the alterations department. "We'll catch up with you once we're finished."

"Here you are, Miss Mauvais," the saleslady said.

Melinda unzipped the garment bag and gave the dress a cursory check. She glanced at Cally, who was leaning over her shoulder for a better look. "What do you think?"

"I think it's *gorgeous*, Melly!" Cally said, running her hand over the fabric. As she did, she noticed that the sales tag was still attached. While Melinda turned to speak to the saleswoman, Cally flipped the tag over and stared at the numbers in front of and behind the comma. The ball gown cost the equivalent of three mortgage payments on the condo she and her mother shared in Williamsburg.

"Would you like to try it on in our dressing room to make sure the alterations are correct?" the saleslady asked.

"That won't be necessary," Melinda replied as she reached into her genuine crocodile Hermès bag and handed the saleslady one of her father's business cards. "I have a seamstress on my staff who can see to it if necessary. Have it sent to this address."

"Right away, Miss Mauvais."

As they headed back to rejoin the Maledetto sisters, Melinda asked the question Cally had been dreading all afternoon: "So, what are you wearing for Rauhnacht?"

Cally paused, trying to decide whether to tell her friend she had not been invited to attend the Grand Ball as one of the year's debutantes. But it felt so good to be accepted as an equal, and she didn't want to do anything that would ruin the moment or embarrass Melinda by pointing out the social chasm between them.

"I've commissioned an original," she replied off-handedly, hoping it would deflect further inquiry.

"Cool! Anyone I know?"

"I don't think so," Cally lied. "She's just getting started, but she's very promising."

"Rauhnacht is all very sexist and medieval, if you ask me," Melinda said with a sigh. "But I can't bash it *too* hard. After all, it's how my parents met. My grandfather Asema came to the Grand Ball here in New York all the way from Suriname to find a husband for my mother."

"Your mom's from South America? Cool! I didn't know that."

"Since my ancestors came to the New World from West Africa instead of Europe, my totem is a panther, not a wolf. Lilith used to tease me for being different."

"She made catty comments, I take it?" Cally said dryly.

Cally and Melinda succeeded in tracking down the twins, who were dutifully sorting through the various gowns in the Vera Wang section.

"Have you found something you like yet?" Cally asked.

"*I* have," Bette said proudly, holding out a sleeveless black gown with a straight skirt.

"I think you have a winner there, Bette!" Cally said approvingly as she eyed the deep V-neck and ruched waistline. "How about you, Bella? What do you think?"

The other twin shook her head. "I don't like showing off so much skin."

"You know, you don't *have* to wear the same evening gown as Bette," Cally reminded her. "In fact, it's considered a big fashion no-no if you *do*."

"But we *always* dress alike," Bella protested. "We're *twins*."

"But that doesn't mean you're the same person. I mean, you two don't have the exact same likes and dislikes, am I right?"

Bella nodded. "She thinks Johnny Depp is cute. I like Orlando Bloom."

"See? That's exactly what I'm talking about!" Cally smiled. "You two might *look* the same on the outside, but on the inside you're different! And it's time you started letting others know that.

"Bella, how about you go pick out a gown that *you* like by the same designer as Bette? That way you can be the same but still be different."

Bella's face suddenly lit up. "I know *just* the one! Wait here—I'll go get it!"

Melinda shook her head in amazement as she watched Bella scamper off. "I've been trying to talk fashion sense into that girl for weeks, and you manage to get through to her in less than a day!"

"This is the one I liked, but *Bette* said it was boring," Bella said, returning with a sleeveless black satin gown with a gathered neckline, a tiny waist, and a full skirt.

"Very nice," Cally said.

"You *really* like it?" Bella asked anxiously. "You don't think it's dull?"

"I think it's very elegant," Cally assured her.

"*Ooh!* You know what would go *perfect* with that?" Melinda exclaimed, her eyes agleam. "These high-heel Azzaro strappy sandals I saw on sale downstairs!" The smile on Melinda's face suddenly disappeared. "Uh-oh. Bitch alert."

"Where?" the twins said in unison, their heads swiveling like radar dishes.

"Over there." Melinda nodded toward the escalators.

Cally felt her stomach knot as she turned to see Lilith Todd, the most popular and feared student at Bathory Academy. Nothing turns a fun afternoon of shopping with the girls into a bummer faster than bumping into someone who has recently tried to kill you.

Unlike the school they attended, Bergdorf's wasn't

an official nonaggression zone. However, acting on vendettas in public, especially when plenty of humans were around, was frowned upon by the Synod. That in and of itself was usually enough to guarantee safe passage. Still, when dealing with someone as vindictive and temperamental as Lilith Todd, anything was possible.

"What do we do?" Bette and Bella whispered in tandem, the same worried look on their identical faces. Given that their father was the sworn enemy of Lilith's father, they were also concerned by Lilith's unexpected appearance.

"There's no reason to get upset," Cally assured them, trying to keep her voice as calm as possible. "We outnumber her, right?"

"Girls like Lilith *never* shop alone," Melinda said, her eyes darting warily about the store. "They're like cobras—if you see one, assume there are others nearby. See what I mean?"

Cally saw Carmen Duivel, in all her red-haired glory, headed in their direction followed by two other girls. The first girl was stork tall and built like a stick insect, with long, strawberry-blond hair drawn back into a partial upsweep. The second girl was short and curvy with sleek black hair worn in a Dutch bob that framed her oval face and accented her Cupid's bow mouth.

"Who are they?" Cally asked.

"Armida Aitken is the tall one, and Lula Lumley

is the short one," Melinda whispered. "They're from established Old Blood families, although nowhere near as powerful as Lilith's. But then, that's how Lilith likes it. It's good to be the queen bee."

"I think we'd better leave," Bella said anxiously.

"We have *every bit* as much right to be here as she does," Cally replied firmly. "We're still in America, even if we are at Bergdorf's. I'm not going to run away simply because Lilith and her posse are in the same building. . . ."

"Well, well, well! Look who it is!" Lilith's voice was loud enough that nearby customers looked up from their shopping. "It's Three-M: Monture, Mauvais, and Maledetto!"

"Shouldn't that be Four-M?" Armida Aitken asked, counting on her fingers. "There's two Maledettos. . . ."

"*No*, because they're interchangeable as far as I'm concerned!" Lilith hissed over her shoulder, irritated at having to explain her joke to someone who was supposed to laugh at it regardless of whether they got it or not.

As Lilith approached, Melinda and the twins stood firm behind Cally, flanking her on either side. Even if they wanted to back down, there was no way of doing so without appearing weak-blooded.

"I didn't know they allowed mongrels in Bergdorf's," Lilith sniffed, looking at Cally as if she were something she'd just scraped off her Fendis.

"They must, because there's a pack of bitches right in front of me," Cally replied.

"Watch your tongue, Monture," Carmen growled. She stepped forward, glaring menacingly, only to freeze as Melinda moved to stand shoulder to shoulder with Cally.

"This isn't school," Lilith snarled. "There aren't any teachers here to intervene on your behalf, New Blood."

"That's funny, I was about to tell *you* the same thing," Cally shot back.

Lilith's eyes narrowed into slivers of blue ice. "You don't belong here, just like you don't belong at Bathory. We're not interested in sharing our territory with a pack of losers, are we, girls?"

"Bergdorf's is *ours!*" Carmen said with a contemptuous toss of her head. "Beat it while you still can."

"Save the Queen of the Damned act for the spods you bully at school," Cally said. "You don't scare us. What are you and your little clique of Vampire American Princesses going to do? Fly around the fragrance counter? Piss on the rugs in the shoe department to mark your turf? Besides, I don't scare easy."

Cally turned and pointed a finger at a mannequin dressed in a cashmere sweater. A spark of bluish-white electricity arced from the tip of her index finger, leaving a scorch mark the size of a dime on the nineteen-hundred-dollar garment.

Armida and Lula gasped and exchanged nervous looks, while Carmen flinched and took an involuntary step back. Lilith didn't blink.

"Now, if you don't mind," Cally said, pushing past Lilith and her entourage, "as much as I would *love* to continue our little conversation, my friends and I are going to check out some shoes."

Cally was on the escalator before she stopped holding her breath. "Praise the Founders that's over with," she gasped.

"You were *incredible*!" Bella and Bette chimed in unison.

"I've never seen *anyone* stand up to Lilith like that!" Melinda laughed. "And she hasn't, either!"

"Do you think the reason she hates me is because she blames me for that friend of hers getting killed—what was her name again?"

"Tanith Graves," Melinda replied. "No, I don't think that's it. Lilith and Tanith were tight, but they weren't *that* tight. If you ask me, I think she's *scared* of you."

"Scared? Of *me*?"

"You can summon lightning just like that!" Melinda said, snapping her fingers. "No one else our age can do anything close! Of *course* she's scared of you!"

Cally glanced back over her shoulder, a worried look on her face. "I dunno, Melly. I think there's more to it than that, but I can't figure out *what*. . . ."

FIND OUT WHAT'S NEXT
FOR CALLY AND LILITH IN